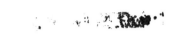

BENICE

AN ADVENTURE OF
LOVE AND FRIENDSHIP

METIN KARAYAKA

ILLUSTRATIONS BY
ROHAN DANIEL EASON

Benice
Copyright © 2018 Metin Karayaka.

ISBN-13: 978-0-9989640-5-8

Karayaka@msn.com

First Edition

1 3 5 7 9 10 8 6 4 2

Printed in the United States of America

To my family and friends – M.K.

THE ISKELE

PROLOGUE

The life of a child in Yalova hasn't changed much since I left. I was once one of the kids returning to the wooden iskele at noon, fishing complete. Some return with their buckets full, some empty, the difference between joy and despair. Whichever it is, I know exactly how they feel; I experienced both feelings many times on this old pier. The iskele was everything to me when I was growing up. It was a sanctuary, a place of hope, and I still find solace here.

I've never been able to explain the importance of the iskele to my friends, but this year they've joined me in Yalova. They're eager to see where I spent my childhood, but I don't know how much they can understand by just walking the streets. It was Orion who wanted to meet with the villagers before tomorrow's big event, and he stands beside me now, smiling at the Yalova kids returning from fishing with their masters.

"Are you enjoying yourself, Orion?" I ask. "You've been asking about the fishermen of Yalova for a long time, and now you're experiencing it all firsthand. Nothing's changed. Fifteen years ago, I was one of these kids."

"Let's go talk to them," Orion says, eager to mingle.

"We need to wait until their master fishermen leave. Don't worry, the kids will stick around. They have chores."

We wait until the kids settle down to clean their fish. Looking at the amount they've caught, I expect a friendly reception, so I let Orion take the lead.

"Hello," he says, approaching one of kids. "It has been a long time since I ate fresh fish. Do you sell your catch?" It's not a bad approach to start a conversation with the kids. I give Orion a thumbs up, and he continues, "I am visiting Yalova for a few days. I'd like to have a fresh barbecue tonight and that tuna you're cleaning looks delicious."

Exactly as I expected, it hasn't taken long for Orion to embarrass himself. Still, I'm enjoying it too much to jump in and help him.

"Welcome to Yalova, sir," the kid says, smiling politely. "This is the best place for fresh fish, but that is not a tuna, it's a barracuda. I will be happy to help you, though; why do you want *this* fish?"

Orion hesitates. "Well, I was thinking we could make some fillets from it."

The kid offers a patient, polite smile. "Sir, we are not in the

Jynx mountains. We don't barbecue fish like steak in Yalova, we grill it. If you want an authentic Yalova experience, you'll want a small fish with lots of bones, not a big fish. The smaller fish taste much better if you grill them right."

"Thanks for the suggestion, but you don't seem to have any small fish."

"You don't have to buy it from me. I would be perfectly happy if you bought it from one of my friends. We want all visitors to Yalova to leave with good memories. I will have my turn next time."

"Okay. Can you help me find the proper fish then?"

"Sure." He yells at his friends, "Hey, guys, bring your buckets over here. I have customers for you. They want fish for grilling."

We're swarmed by eager kids. Orion is happy with the attention, and I'm happy to be reliving my childhood memories.

"How can we help, Cem?"

"Just put your buckets there, I will select the fish for them."

Cem digs through his friends' buckets and selects a few fish. He picks different sizes and shapes. To Orion, I'm sure there appears to be no rhyme or reason to his selection process.

"I selected the best catch of the day. Two red snappers, three tilapia, and two red fish. I will clean and prepare these fish for you. When you grill them, just sprinkle a pinch of thyme and put lemon wedges on them. Please don't add anything else. This isn't barbecue meat."

This little fish monger knows exactly what he's doing. While I pay the kids, Orion continues his conversation with Cem.

"It looks like you caught lots of fish today, but you still seem a little upset. What's going on?"

"You're wrong about the size of our haul," Cem says, not looking up. "This is typical for us, sir. Most of us are really good fishermen. But yes, we're upset. We just found out the iskele will be closed for a private party tomorrow. We can't even come near. That's a whole day's fishing lost!"

"Well, it's just one day," Orion replies. "You can go fishing the day after."

Orion doesn't understand. I raise an eyebrow to show my disapproval, but Cem is livid. He stops cleaning the fish and jumps up to confront Orion.

"What are you talking about? Our survival depends on the fish we catch!"

"Cem," I say, "please excuse my friend. I certainly understand how you feel."

What's true for him was once true for me. When I was his age, I fought for every ounce of fish to support my family.

"No, I don't think you can, sir. You aren't from here. Come to think of it, you're probably the reason we aren't going fishing tomorrow. Am I right?"

"Um," I murmur, reluctantly accepting our guilt, "yes, you *are* correct. We're the reason your fishing will be interrupted.

But you're wrong about something else. I *did* grow up in this town. When I was your age, I was a fisherman too. I totally get why you're upset. Kids have been coming to this spot at sunrise for as long as I can remember."

"So, you knew our traditions and still arranged a party at sunrise?" Cem asks, seeing my guilt and seizing his opportunity. "Couldn't you have planned your party for later in the day, after we've finished our fishing? I was counting on making money tomorrow. You took our money. You should pay us back somehow."

I smile and gladly oblige, paying the kids more than their losses. It's an expensive icebreaker, but I don't mind. I wanted to show Orion a glimpse of my childhood, and the kids are doing a heck of a job at that. As more kids start to gather around, hands out, I feel like I finally have enough of an audience to ask my real question.

"Have you ever heard of a fisherman named Mr. Ben?"

"Of course!" one boy shouts. "When my dad was my age, Mr. Ben taught him how to fish. My father told me that Mr. Ben still holds the record for the biggest fish ever caught in Yalova."

"Mr. Ben taught my father how to fish, too," says another kid. "He's a legend around here."

"No, sir, he wasn't a fisherman," says another kid, stepping forward. "He was a pirate!"

Another kid jumps in to refute this, and yet another answers back.

"These kids are wrong, sir. He was a monster! My father knew he was a pirate, and he never went fishing with him."

"That's a lie," growls an older child. "Shut up! Your father is as stupid as you are. He didn't know what he was missing. Mr. Ben was kind, and he loved all the kids of Yalova."

Eager to avoid a fight, I jump in.

"Whoa there, everyone. Let's all just calm down. Do you know where Mr. Ben is now? What happened to him?"

"He isn't in Yalova anymore, sir. He went fishing a long time ago and never came back. We don't know what happened, but his empty boat washed ashore one month after he left town. I believe he still lives on the high seas. He'll be back, one day."

Goosebumps shoot up my arms. I've been back many times since my childhood, but nobody ever mentioned recovering Mr. Ben's boat.

"Can you show me his boat?" I ask the kids.

"Sure," says Cem, "but it'll cost you."

"Okay, okay," I say, laughing at his hustle. "I'll pay – so long as you aren't lying."

Following Cem and the gang of Yalova kids, I walk underneath the iskele, weaving between its supports. When we reach a tarp-covered boat, the gang trailing behind us fans out, surrounding us. A few of Cem's friends rush to help him remove the tarp, and I feel Orion's hand on my shoulder, bracing me for disappointment. As the tarp falls away, I can't believe my eyes. Its bright red colors have faded, and it's smaller than I remember, but this is *Eyass*, Mr. Ben's boat.

"It's been sitting here ever since it was found. I don't think anybody will care if you want to take it. It's just rotting, anyway."

"I will definitely take care of *Eyass*, yes. This boat witnessed so many important events in my life."

I step back, making room for Orion. He's even happier to see *Eyass* than I am, especially because it's for the first time. I've told him so many stories about this boat.

"This is amazing, Levend," he says. "We should show *Eyass* to everyone tomorrow. I'm sure they'll enjoy it."

I make a few circles around *Eyass,* touching its keel and caressing the beautiful ironwork nameplate on its side. Truly ecstatic, I sit inside the boat and pretend to cast my fishing line. Having absorbed as much of the moment as I can, I turn my attention back to the kids. I can see in their eyes that they're puzzled as to why this old boat has made me behave so strangely.

"I have a confession to make," I admit. "I went fishing with Mr. Ben in this boat many, many times." The kids aren't impressed; after all, Mr. Ben taught almost all of their fathers to fish in this very boat. Happily, I'm not done. "Not only that; I was in it with Mr. Ben when he left Yalova."

That gets a better reaction. After a moment of silence, awe-struck kids begin battering me with questions.

"Is he still alive?"

"Is he a good guy?"

"Is he a pirate?"

"Where is he now?"

"When is he coming back?"

"Hold on, hold on!" I shout, but nobody seems to hear me. "Kids, calm down, please!"

They still don't respond, and I'm left with no choice but to wait out the chatter. It takes a few minutes.

"If you want to see Mr. Ben, come to the party tomorrow. I can't guarantee you'll see him in person, but you'll definitely see his legacy."

The kids respond with deafening cheers.

"Come on, Mr. Levend," shouts Cem. "We can't wait until tomorrow. You have to tell us Mr. Ben's story. We're not going to let you go anywhere until you've told us everything you know about him."

I consider the boy's words. I suppose I do owe them for leading me to the boat.

"Sit down, Orion," I say. "I think we should spend this beautiful afternoon at the iskele." Then, I turn my attention to the kids. "Make a circle around me and Mr. Orion. You're going to hear the most amazing story of love and friendship ever told."

BARBAROSSA AND LEVEND

CHAPTER ONE

FISHERMEN
OF YALOVA

When I was growing up, our empire was in chaos. The harmony among the three ancient tribes – the Orhuns, the Nevars, and the Jynxes – died with King Soltun, and many of our institutions followed. The Nevars were quick to seize control, setting cruel Korsan upon the throne, but the Jynxes refused to recognize his claim, taking to the high seas. They were decried as pirates and, hounded by their former countrymen, quickly adopted the violence and lawlessness of that label. The worst of them became half-legend, and children swapped stories of fearsome figures like terrible Jamoka and fearsome BarbaRossa. Though Korsan claimed he ruled the empire, the truth was that he was the king only of the land,

and Jamoka's pirates ruled the seas. As the civil war raged, there were fewer and fewer safe places in the empire. Peaceful refugees from all tribes, especially the elderly, women, and children, descended on Yalova in their fishing boats. Yalova became a melting pot for Orhuns, Nevars, and Jynxes. By the time of my childhood, you could no longer tell who was born in Yalova and who was a refugee.

The elderly fished early in the morning and played backgammon at coffee shops in the afternoon. Fishing was the bond between the old refugees and the young Yalova kids, and if we kids were willing to lend a hand, we'd often be taken out onto the water. At the time, I didn't understand why they were so happy to take us out, but it was simple, really. They just wanted to tell us about their life experiences and nurture us as we grew. They remembered a time of unity and hoped to keep it alive in our hearts. I enjoyed spending time with the fishermen at the iskele, relaxing by the ocean and catching fish. I couldn't fish during the winter, but over the summer I would go on three or four excursions a week, catching fish early in the morning and selling them at the bazaar in the afternoon. The more fish I caught, the more money I made. It was enough to buy my school supplies and more, which helped me support Auntie Aysun, who raised my sister Ayshin and me on little income.

It was easy for kids to get out on the water; there were lots of fishermen and not enough eager pairs of ears for each. Most of

them weren't even interested in the fish, more eager for somebody to talk to and who would help out with their chores. It
was an unwritten rule that if they accepted you as a fishing
partner, you got to keep the fish.

My morning routine was to wake up before sunrise, go to
the iskele before the other kids arrived, and hook up with the
best fisherman available that day. They'd never ask for company; you had to ask them and bring along a bucket to carry
your fish. That was it, though – they didn't want to deal with
kids' messy fishing gear, so there was no need to bring fishing
poles or bait. We didn't need any kind of prior agreement; if
the fisherman agreed to take you, you started to help with the
boat, prepared some bait, and then off you went. The more fish
we caught, the more money I made. I was good at fishing, and
I was never rejected by any of the fishermen. They liked me
because I always cleaned the boat afterwards, and I was easy to
talk to.

Every day, I stuck around to watch the remaining fishermen
come back to the iskele, counting up their fish to find out who
was the best. Oddly enough, the best fisherman, Mr. Ben, never
brought a single fish back to shore. He always caught-and-re-
leased. Still, everybody in town knew he was the best.

He knew how to read the ocean. Sometimes he sailed far
away to deep waters, sometimes he would stay in the shallows.
Sometimes he fished on the surface with small bait, sometimes

he used big hooks to fish on the ocean floor. Sometimes he stayed in one spot, sometimes he trolled his boat. His fishing methods varied, but he always sailed alone, away from the other fishermen. If somebody followed him, trying to ride his coattails to a better fishing spot, he pushed them away. So the other fishermen watched him from a distance, shaking their heads as he caught more and bigger fish than they could hope for, only to release them.

Though they knew Mr. Ben was the best fisherman, not many people liked him, and I didn't blame them. He'd already been in Yalova a couple of years, but he rarely talked to anybody. I never even saw him greet someone. At first, I wondered if he was shy or embarrassed, because he was an unusual-looking man. At some point in his life, he had lost not just an eye, but also a hand and a leg. He wore an eyepatch, and had been fitted with a sharp metal hook and a sturdy wooden leg. On top of all this, he had a pet parrot.

You guessed it! Everybody thought Mr. Ben was a pirate, and many believed he was hiding from his enemies. Villagers wanted to kick him out of town and kids were scared to even be near his boat. There were so many rumors. Some believed that he used kids as bait, or that he poked kids' eyeballs out, trying to find a fitting replacement for the one he'd lost.

There came a time when Mr. Ben was the only fisherman I'd never sailed with. I'd imagined it, of course, figuring that the catch from one day of fishing with him would be equal to three days with the next best fisherman. That is, if we kept the fish, which I would insist on, though I knew I'd go with him even if he refused.

Every morning, at the iskele, his boat was like a magnet. I circled around all the boats with the other kids, but I always found myself next to his. Like any other fourteen-year-old kid, I was too scared to talk to him, but I still wanted to learn from the best.

One morning, I was watching Mr. Ben sharpen his knives and imagining he was preparing to chop up some kids. As usual, I hadn't said a word, but as I turned around to look for a different fisherman, I felt cold metal on my shoulder.

I froze.

"Do you want to go fishing with me?" asked a voice behind me. I was so scared that I couldn't swallow; I couldn't even breathe.

"Yes," I whispered, giving the only answer I believed he would accept.

"What's your name?"

"My name is Levend."

"Well, you've been circling my boat almost all summer, Levend."

I turned around. Mr. Ben was looking at me, but he wasn't smiling. He didn't look inviting, though he did look as if he was at least trying to be polite – quite an effort for a one-eyed man holding a knife.

"I've packed up all my gear," he said, "I've sharpened all my knives, and I'm ready to go. This is your first and last chance to come with me."

"You're prepared all right," I said, backing away a few steps. It suddenly occurred to me that, if I got in the boat, I'd be alone with him in the middle of the sea. Even if I screamed at the top of my lungs, nobody would hear me.

I turned around, intent on running away as fast as I could. Too late! He gestured toward the boat with his big knife.

"Get in the boat, then."

"Are you going to teach me how to fish?" I whispered.

"Sure," he replied, cracking a smile. "I'll teach you how to fish, if there's time."

Reluctantly, I got into the boat. He jumped in after me and started to sail away from the beach. It didn't take long for us to reach the deep sea. There were other fishermen around us, so I started to feel a little safer.

"Are we going to fish here?" I asked.

"No. We'll go to my secret place." He pointed to the fisher-men around us. "These men are fools; there are no fish here today."

"How do you know, Mr. Ben?"

"I can hear the tiniest ripples of the ocean, I can read the sun's reflection, and I can sense the wind on my skin. I'm an old-school fisherman. The ocean always tells me where the fish are."

He wasn't bragging; he meant what he said, and I was impressed.

"I'm telling you," Mr. Ben continued, "there are no fish here today. To find some, we'll have to go to my secret place."

This was good news and bad news. Good news because we might catch lots of fish, but bad news because the nearest person would be miles away, and Mr. Ben had just sharpened his knives! Although catching extra fish was appealing, I didn't want to die for it. I tried to use my charm to talk him out of going to his secret place.

"Oh, Mr. Ben, I'm okay if we catch fewer fish. All I wanted today was to learn how to fish. We can go to the secret place another time. Wouldn't it be better if I just learn fishing here? After my training, we can go to that secret place. It's probably far away, right?"

He paused a moment, then said, "You have a point, Levend, but you may never have a chance to come fishing with me again."

Hoppalaa! I was definitely about to become fish food!

We started to speed away from the other fishermen. He was heading for Heybeliada, an island in the middle of the Marmara Sea.

"Please, I'm just a little kid!"

I was about to cry.

With an evil grin on his face, he said, "I know you're a little kid, Levend, and you have tender muscles. You agreed to come fishing with me, right? That means you have to follow the captain's rules while you're on his ship."

He was enjoying torturing me with his words, but I corrected him anyway.

"This isn't a ship, it's only a fishing boat, and a small one at that!"

"Sorry," he chuckled, "old habits die hard."

Why had he called his little boat a ship? Why had he mentioned my tender muscles? All I could think was that he would use me as fish bait. Why didn't he just kill me and get it over with? My world started to collapse, and then, without warning, there was only darkness.

TURTLE POKE

CHAPTER TWO

FISHING WITH MR. BEN

opened my eyes, not knowing how long I'd been out. I couldn't move, and I quickly realized that my hands and feet were tied down to the boat. Squinting against the glare of the sun, I saw Mr. Ben. He was holding one of his biggest knives, rubbing it against his hook to create a horrible screech.

"Am I alive?" I asked.

"Yes. For now," said Mr. Ben.

I was ready to scream, *Untie me right now!*, but I knew it wouldn't help.

Instead, I asked, "What's going to happen to me now?"

"Don't worry your little head about that," he said. "I know you're uncomfortable, but I'll fix that in just a few minutes. I'm good with a knife, it'll be an easy job. But let me anchor the boat first. Then, I can start preparing bait."

Without missing a step, he dropped anchor.

He was going to chop me up for bait! Mr. Ben came closer, a

knife in one hand and a sharp hook for the other. He kneeled, pinning my chest with the curved side of his hook. He lifted up his knife, brought it close to my throat, and I looked him in the eye. Looking at me like I was prey, he cut the rope from my feet. Then, he cut the rope from my hands.

I stood slowly, confused and dizzy, and asked, "Why did you tie me down?"

"You didn't leave me any choice," he said. "I needed to steer the boat, but I couldn't be sure you wouldn't fall overboard."

"Oh," I mumbled, "I thought you were going to make me fish bait."

I thought he'd scare away the fish, he laughed so loud! He had definitely enjoyed scaring me.

"Where did you get that idea?" he asked eventually.

"Well… you kind of look like a pirate," I replied.

"A pirate! Don't you know most of the pirates are Jynx? I'm an Orhun, just like you."

I let out a big sigh of relief, gathering the courage to ask him a few more questions.

"Well, Ben, I mean *Mr.* Ben, there were a lot of rumors about you. I have a few questions I've been dying to ask since the first day I saw you at the iskele. I want to learn the truth from you instead of learning from other people."

"And I want to know all about you as well. Maybe we will become good friends. You can ask me anything you want."

I finally had my chance; I was determined to make him admit he used to be a pirate.

"Did you ever work for King Korsan or Jamoka?"

"No. I would never work for either one of those evil men. Their cruel ways brought chaos to our empire. I am not that kind of person."

"But you have a lot of battle scars."

"What battle scars?"

"You're wearing an eyepatch. What happened to your eye?"

"Well," he began, "I lost my eye when I was seven years old. While playing in the sand, I found a turtle. I proudly showed my catch to my friends, intending to take it home and make it my pet. One of my friends asked me, 'What color are its eyes?' I held the turtle by its sides, trying to catch a glimpse, but his head was hunkered down inside his shell. My friend said, 'If we put a stick in his bottom, he might pop his head out! Then you can see the color of his eyes.' I thought it was a great idea, and my friend jabbed the turtle with a stick. Zing! The turtle's head came out. But, darn it, he was gone too quickly for me to see the color of his eyes. I told my friend to do it again. This time, I got closer to the turtle. My friend pushed the stick again.

"Zing! Head out again. I could see his purple eyes. 'Neat,' I said, but the turtle didn't agree. He had tolerated the first stick, but not the second. He snapped one of my eyeballs clear out. I swear I heard him say, 'Zing!' I learned later that he was a snapping turtle." He flipped his eyepatch. "So, I've been missing an eye for almost my entire life. What else do you want to know?"

The hole made me squeamish. I had to gather myself for a second question.

"One of your hands is a hook. How did that happen?"

"Which hook?" he asked.

"The one you're wearing on your hand, of course! How did you lose your hand? I bet during a sword fight."

"I never used a sword in my life," Mr. Ben replied. "I lost my hand a long time ago, as well. I was eight years old, almost one year after I lost my eye. I'm so used to it, I barely even remember I'm wearing a hook."

"I'd love to hear what happened to your hand, Mr. Ben," I said, preparing to hear another lie.

"I lost my hand during my first deep-sea fishing trip," he explained. "I got a bite on my fishing line. We fought for almost two hours to reel the fish in. In the end, I won the fight, and the fish gave up. When we pulled it aboard, it was a small shark, about four feet long."

"What does this have to do with your hand?" I asked.

"Well, I forgot to mention to you that I was the bait!"

"I don't understand."

"I was sitting on the side of the boat with my fishing pole. Since I only had one eye, my peripheral vision wasn't very good.

I couldn't judge where the edge of the boat was, and I fell into the water with my fishing pole. Luckily, the fishhook was stuck in the boat, and I was able to hold on to the pole. The captain secured the hook and shouted that as long as I held on, they could reel me in. I held the pole in one hand and felt a stinging pain in the other.

"I looked out of the corner of my eye and saw a shark had bitten me and was trying to pull me away from the boat! I was kicking and screaming, gripping the fishing pole with my other hand the whole time. The captain and his crew were trying to pull me in, and I knew that if I released that fishing pole, I would be dead in the water. They finally managed to reel me in, but unfortunately the shark came with me and, with one last bite, it swallowed my hand. They wrapped my stump with towels and, several years later, I got this hook. I know how to use it now. Although I can't scratch my face, it has some advantages. I can open bottles with it!" He caught his breath and asked, "Now, curious boy, any other questions?"

"What a big whopper," I whispered to myself. I tried to make a joke. "Can you juggle?"

"Ha! Go ahead, little one, make fun. I'm used to it. People ask me all sorts of questions, 'How do you go to the bathroom?' or 'Can you pick out your boogers?' Nobody has ever asked me about juggling before, but I *have* tried it in the past. Juggling bean bags wasn't too difficult, but I ripped holes in a few before

I learned how to safely catch them. Do you know how many beans there are in a bean bag?"

I shook my head.

"Lots," he said.

"I had a third question for you, but I think I already have an answer for it, so I'm not going to ask."

"Go ahead. You can ask me any question you like. I'm starting to enjoy your company."

"Well, an alligator snapped your leg off when you were nine years old, right?"

"How did you know that? How did you guess?"

I just saved you from telling another lie, I thought to myself. Now, I was convinced that he had definitely been a pirate. He'd probably lost his hand and leg during a raid. Despite all that, I couldn't resist asking about the parrot.

"What about the parrot, Mr. Ben? How did you get it?"

"Everybody needs a parrot, Levend! Unfortunately, my parrot, Toy, isn't very smart. She rarely says any words."

I threw my hands up in the air. He had answers for everything, and none of them were satisfying.

"I have no more questions, Mr. Ben. Can we start fishing now?"

"Let's roll," he laughed. "Now, a good fisherman should always be concerned with finding a good spot. Otherwise, you're wasting your time. After finding the right place, you need to focus on other factors. The time of day needs to be right; the wind has to be right; the bait has to be right; everything needs to be perfect. I can teach you how to read the sea in theory, but it will take you a long time to be any good at it. But never mind the small steps; I already took care of finding a good location. The second step is to prepare your gear and bait."

He patiently showed me how to prepare tackles and lures for different types and sizes of fish and basket-traps for lobsters. Everything he did had purpose; he knew exactly what to do, not wasting a moment. Although he shied away from talking to anybody at the iskele, he turned out to be quite a good teacher. On top of that, he seemed to be enjoying teaching me, and I was certainly learning a lot. Once we were ready, we cast our first lines.

Boom! I caught a blowfish in the first minute. I reeled it in and took it off the hook.

"Mr. Ben," I asked, gently holding out the fish, "may I—"

"You can keep the fish," he interrupted. "I know you want to make some money. I never wanted to keep the fish, because I'm alone, and I eat very little. I don't need the money, either. I fish for fun, but I don't mind if you take that baby home."

My eyes sparkled. *All of this suffering is paying off,* I thought. I put the blowfish in the bucket, then hooked my next bait and returned to fishing. I shot Mr. Ben a big smile.

"Those amateurs on the shore will see what a real fisherman

can do now," I crowed. "Did you know, Mr. Ben, everybody is so curious about how many fish you can catch in a day?"

"Of course I know. When we bring our haul to shore today, they can stop gossiping about it. Keep fishing."

My next catch was a huge stingray, then another, then another. I reeled fish in all day long.

It turned out to be a fantastic day. Mr. Ben was friendly, made good jokes, and taught me a lot about fishing. Most importantly, I wasn't used as bait. I started to think Mr. Ben wasn't a pirate after all. Maybe he'd just had a string of bad luck in his childhood. I could barely imagine someone losing an eye, and then a hand, and then a foot – all within three years. Yikes!

We were done by noon, so we packed up and headed back to town. As we sailed, I could feel the breeze on my face. I had started the boat trip fearing for my life and ended up trusting Mr. Ben with it. I was so tired that I closed my eyes and started to fall asleep. I knew that Mr. Ben wouldn't let me fall into the sea.

ELEVEN BUCKETS OF FISH

CHAPTER THREE

ELEVEN BUCKETS OF FISH

When we got closer to shore, I saw lots of activity at the iskele.

"Something's wrong," I told Mr. Ben. "Look at all those people!"

Mr. Ben was calmer than me, but I could still tell he was worried. As we got closer, the noise grew louder.

"They're coming!" a woman screamed.

"Who's coming?" I asked. "What's going on, Mr. Ben?"

We continued to slowly approach the iskele.

"He's alive!" someone yelled.

"I can see with my binoculars!" called a kid's voice, but not one I recognized. "Oh my gosh, Levend's ears are missing! I bet that monster chopped them off and used them as fish bait."

We got closer, and I saw my sister Ayshin and her best friends Zhu Zhu and Zhen Zhen in the crowd.

"Levend! Oh, I'm glad you're back. I love you even without your ears!" Ayshin was crying. "I want my GeGe back!"

"Who is GeGe?" asked Mr. Ben.

"Um… I am," I replied. In that moment, I wished my ears *were* gone, because they were burning with embarrassment. "That's just what she calls me instead of Little Brother."

It was at that moment that Mr. Ben and I realized they were waiting for us. As soon as I jumped out of the boat, they surrounded me and started searching for injuries. The kid with the binoculars and the bad eyesight adjusted his glasses and revised the news.

"Hey, everybody, Levend still has both ears!"

Members of the militia jumped on Mr. Ben. They finally had an excuse to arrest him! They told him that he didn't have permission to take a kid fishing, and that he would be charged with kidnapping. From what they said, it sounded as if he could be locked away for the rest of his life. I wriggled out of Ayshin's arms and yelled at everybody to stop talking.

"*Hey!* He's no pirate!"

Shocked, the crowd went quiet, and I asked my best friends to find buckets and come with me to the boat. We jumped in the boat and filled eleven buckets with fish. The buckets were so heavy that the kids we were barely able to carry them. We laid down all the fish, side-by-side, and I could hear everybody whispering.

"How did a little boy and an old man catch so many fish? Impossible!"

I climbed onto the boat's prow and grabbed a cone that the militia used to make their voices louder.

"Calm down, everybody," I boomed. "First of all, I asked Mr. Ben to take me fishing. He didn't kidnap me. I begged him to take me fishing and teach me his tricks. Do you see how many fish we caught? He's the best fisherman in Yalova, and I'm happy I went fishing with him. He's actually a good guy, too. You don't have to be scared of him anymore! As a gesture of our good intentions, Mr. Ben and I won't take any of the fish home today, except for the stingray. I'm taking the stingray! The rest of the fish will be given to all of you. There are even more fish in the boat."

The crowd relaxed; everybody would get something, but I didn't stop there.

"Mr. Ben has also agreed to teach kids who want to improve their fishing skills. Can you imagine all of Yalova's kids learning how to fish like this? What a great service to our community!"

Mr. Ben hadn't expected that. I could tell he was about to object, but then he must have realized that his hands were handcuffed and he was surrounded by the militia. His silence was enough, and the militia chief unlocked the handcuffs.

"You are officially on probation until you prove as good as your word. Report to the iskele tomorrow morning and start teaching the kids. I don't want to see you out on the water by yourself!"

The punishment was getting worse for Mr. Ben.

"What? I didn't do anything to lose my freedom to go fishing by myself."

"Don't you get it, Mr. Ben? We don't like cold souls in this town. I don't know, and I don't care, what you did before coming to Yalova, but when you are in our town, you have to abide by our rules. Otherwise, I will find a way to put you in jail."

Mr. Ben stared at me and reluctantly agreed.

"Don't worry, Mr. Ben," I said, regretting that I'd put him in such a bad position. "I'll come fishing with you ev—"

Just before I finished my sentence, Auntie Aysun smacked me on the head.

"No, you are not going with him every day!"

With all the fuss over, the crowd dispersed, but the villagers still weren't ready to accept Mr. Ben. I spent the rest of the summer convincing my friends to go fishing with Mr. Ben. At first, the kids were confused. Should they be happy about fishing with a pirate? Most kids refused to go out with Mr. Ben at first, but the brave ones could bring home a huge haul. Gradually, kids started to like Mr. Ben. Even the idea that he looked like a scary pirate, true though it was, faded away.

REPAIRING EYASS

CHAPTER FOUR

HIDDEN ICE

Although the militia never officially lifted his probation, Mr. Ben's status in the town started to change. By the end of summer, someone went fishing with him almost every day, but there was still a small stab of panic when they got far from the shore. He had been terrifying for so long that, no matter how much you knew about him, you felt just a little scared. Unfortunately, Auntie Aysun insisted I had scared her enough with my first voyage, so it was some time before I set sail with Mr. Ben again.

Sure enough, each kid caught their share of fish, but nobody was able to catch as many as I had. I heard that Mr. Ben didn't take any other kid to his secret fishing place, and I decided that meant it was *our* secret place from now on.

In time, there were so many kids who wanted to fish with Mr. Ben that he had to select them through a contest. Whoever had the cleverest rhyme was chosen. Eventually, I won with:

Mr. Ben, Mr. Ben,
  come out of your den.
I brought you a dish,
  you should catch me a fish.

I brought his favorite cookies in a dish, and he chose me for the second time. I wasn't as scared this time, and I asked him to take us to the secret place again.

Instead of going to his boat, he took me to his shed. He gave half of the cookies to Toy, sat on his rocking chair, and started to eat his share while sipping hot tea and watching Toy nibble at her cookies.

"Come sit with me and enjoy the show. You can have some of my cookies too."

It would have been an understatement to call Toy dumb! She was trying to hold a cookie with her wings like a human and failing miserably. I tried to teach Toy how to break the cookies with her beak, but that was a futile effort. Mr. Ben was having fun.

"Do you want to come tomorrow to watch Toy drink soup with a spoon? That's an even better show."

The bird was also incredibly stubborn. It took a long time for Toy to finish the cookies, and I think she wasted more than half of them. I had to admit it was hilarious to watch Toy, but we were losing time. Mr. Ben did not appear to have any intention of going fishing.

"Why are we wasting the early morning breeze in your shed? Shouldn't we be sailing by now?" I asked.

"It's your lucky day, Levend," he said. "We aren't going out on the water. Today, we need to take care of *Eyass*, my boat, and I'm going to teach you how to be a sailor."

"I didn't know your boat had a name, Mr. Ben. What does Eyass mean?"

"You really don't know, Levend? A baby falcon is called an 'eyass'."

"That's a cute name for a fishing boat," I said, but I wasn't thrilled that we weren't going out to sea. "Why are we staying on land to learn how to be a sailor? I thought the best way to be a fisherman was to be out there, on the ocean?"

"Anybody can be a fisherman, but not everybody can be a sailor. I'm a sailor first and a fisherman second. Trust me, there's no end to a sailor's horizon. Besides, I like you and I want you to be successful when you grow up. Now, jump on *Eyass* and show me how to steer the boat to starboard."

I didn't know what starboard meant, so I turned the rudder to the left. He got in the boat and shoved the rudder to the right.

"I guess your lesson starts right now," he chuckled. "Now, sit and look toward the front of *Eyass*. What you're looking at is the 'bow' of the boat, behind you is the 'stern', the right-hand side is 'starboard', and the left-hand side is 'port'. When the boat swings side to side, it's called 'roll'. When the boat rocks front and back, it's called 'pitch'; and when the boat rotates, it's called 'yaw'."

"That's too much information, Mr. Ben."

"Well, you have to start somewhere. Every seaman, whether a pirate or the admiral of a navy fleet, uses these terms. An admiral never tells his marines to go to the back of the ship; he tells them to go 'aft'. A pirate never turns his ship to the left; he always turns the ship to 'port'. You use these terms regardless of the ship's size. You can use them for a rowboat, or you can use them for a ship on the ocean."

"Wow! I have a lot to learn."

"Now, enough of that sailor jargon," he declared. "If you want to be a sailor, you have to love and respect your boat. Let's take care of *Eyass* so she can take care of us."

I started to see the big picture; Mr. Ben was right, if you didn't take care of your boat, you wouldn't be able to return from a fishing trip.

"So, what's next, Mr. Ben?"

"Today, we're going to paint *Eyass*."

"*Eyass* looks fine to me. Why do we need to paint it?" I asked. I could tell I'd said something inappropriate by the way he looked at me.

"Come closer. Look at the wooden planks. What do you see?"

"Nothing special."

"Now, put your hand underneath the boat and touch the paint. Do you feel where it's bumpy? When water gets under the paint, the planks start to rot. If we don't maintain it, *Eyass* will start to leak."

"So you can find damage you can't even see? What do we need to do?"

"We need to strip the paint from the damaged areas by sanding it. Then, we repaint it bright red."

"Why bright red?"

"Good question. The boat's color needs to be as bright as possible. That way, it reflects the sun when we're on the ocean, and the boat won't be as hot. On top of that, we'll be easy to see. As for choosing red... well, *Eyass* may only be a young bird, but there is no greater power than falcon's blood."

It was hard work to scrape the old paint from the wooden planks. We spent the entire morning scraping and then repainting the boat. While I was finishing up the last of the painting, Mr. Ben started a fire pit. I found that odd, because it was a hot summer's day. When I finished my painting, the fire was really high, and Mr. Ben was laying metal tools next to the pit.

"What's going on, Mr. Ben? Are we going to make some fishing equipment from those metal pieces?"

Mr. Ben rolled his eyes. "These are blacksmith's tools. Take a look at *Eyass* and tell me what's missing."

"It looks perfect to me."

"It ain't so, Levend. *Eyass* is missing its name."

He carefully positioned the anvil next to the fire, placing some pieces of metal on the flames. I was curious, but he just waited. Eventually, the metal pieces turned red hot.

He turned to me and said, "It's time!"

"Time for what?" I asked.

"Time to make a nameplate for *Eyass*."

I held my breath as he stuck his hook into the fire and picked up one of the glowing pieces of metal. He put it on the anvil and started pounding on it with a huge hammer. He was extremely skillful, and within just a few minutes, I could see the letters "E" and "Y" taking shape. Before too long, "EYASS" was ready. He put the nameplate in the fire again. We waited until the metal started to glow, then he turned to me.

"You will put the final touches on *Eyass*."

I was shocked by the invitation but thrilled at the prospect of crafting something with fire.

"What do you want me to do?" I asked. "I can't stick my arm in the fire, and I can't lift that heavy hammer!"

"Relax," he said. "I'll lift the nameplate from the fire with my hook. You'll put the final touches on with a small hammer. Trust me, it's a two-man job at this point. The master blacksmith orients the nameplate, and his skillful apprentice hammers it."

I can't tell you how much I enjoyed creating something

beautiful from a dull metal bar. When we finished, we polished the nameplate and attached it to the boat. I think Mr. Ben enjoyed teaching me his craft. At one point, our eyes connected, and he looked at me with a warm smile.

I smiled back, unable to resist asking, "Mr. Ben, did you ever have a family?"

He stayed silent for a few seconds, though it felt like ten minutes, and then he looked at me again. I gave him a comforting smile, and he took a deep breath.

"Yes, my dear, I had a family once."

I opened my eyes wider, giving him my full attention, but he fell silent.

"Mr. Ben," I said, "it's okay if you don't want to talk about it."

"No, no, I'm not afraid of talking about it. To tell you the truth, you look a lot like my son." Mr. Ben reached into his chest pocket and carefully removed a picture. "This is my son when he was a little younger than you."

He choked up a little.

"Wow, he does look like me! Where does he live now?"

"He passed away. I never even saw him. The only thing I have of him is this picture."

"How did you get the picture?"

"I got it from a Jynx named Zamora."

"Zamora must be a good friend."

"No, Levend, he's no such thing. Actually, he's about as bad of a person as one can be. He's definitely not my friend."

"I never met my father, either," I said, moving toward him with teary eyes and giving him a hug. "I know exactly how you feel."

I sat on his lap, now completely unafraid. It was clearly a difficult subject for Mr. Ben, and I didn't want to bother him any further. In fact, I wanted to cheer him up, so I changed the subject.

"Mr. Ben, I think we haven't been respectful to you."

"Who hasn't been respectful to me?"

"The entire town."

"Why do you think that? You kids certainly made me feel welcome."

"Well, we've been calling you by your first name ever since we met you. We should call you by your last name. I don't think anybody knows your last name. What is it?"

He paused for a long time, and again I was confused. Surely this wasn't a hard question.

"It's been a long time since anybody asked me my last name," he said.

"You're not so old that you can't remember it, are you?" I asked.

"Of course I remember my last name, you silly boy!" he replied. "My last name is…" He became emotional again and couldn't complete his sentence. He closed his eyes. "My last name is Ice."

"Okay, I will start calling you 'Mr. Ice' from now on, Mr. Ben Ice."

He laughed, and I laughed too. Already, I was thinking up another rhyme for Mr. Ice and looking forward to my next visit.

SEABUBBLE

CHAPTER FIVE

SEABUBBLES

I t was a long time before I had another chance to fish with Mr. Ice, and I took up some hobbies in the meantime. I started to play soccer on the field next to Alaaddin's rubber factory, which was near our neighborhood.

The factory was a nasty place – perhaps the filthiest in the empire. Alaaddin was a cunning man, and he knew that the people of Yalova would put up with a lot to avoid the government's attention. Exactly what he was doing in his factory was a mystery. We rarely saw a customer going into the building, and he was always eager to pay good money for any unusual sea creatures we caught. Many of us kids thought that the whole thing was probably a cover for witchcraft. He burned rubber all day long, constantly pumping out black smoke and slimy goo, knowing that we would never report him. The people of Yalova challenged him sometimes, and he'd behave a little better afterwards, but soon he'd be back to dumping his rubber trash in the neighborhood and experimenting with toxic chemicals. It was part of life in Yalova, and we coped the best we could, especially considering that the best soccer fields were right next to the factory.

One day, I was hanging out with some other kids after a game, playing around near an abandoned well. Tired, I sat down on the well's edge and began thinking about my next trip out with Mr. Ice. I was composing a rhyme he might like when somebody bumped into me. I grabbed for safety, but it was too late, and I fell backwards into the darkness of the well!

Fortunately, it wasn't a dry well, but neither was it filled with water. I landed in a huge puddle of disgusting slime, screaming and yelling for my friends to save me. They went to find a rope, and after nearly two hours of chaos, finally pulled me out. I was covered with slime, but there was no water nearby to clean myself, so I had to walk all the way home covered in the green goo.

When I arrived home, Auntie Aysun was angry at me, of course.

"You've been getting into trouble again, haven't you? I told you so many times not to play near Alaaddin's factory! It's dangerous; that place doesn't exactly make candy! Don't come inside without cleaning yourself. Go to the backyard, and don't make a mess."

"I'll try," I said.

Ayshin, Zhu Zhu, and Zhen Zhen were in the backyard, painting. At that time, elsewhere in the empire, it would have been an unusual sight to see two Nevars playing with my Orhun sister. Thankfully, Yalova's seclusion allowed us to live in imitation of the old peace, although that didn't mean any of them went easy on me! As soon as they saw me covered in green slime, they started laughing. They genuinely enjoyed it when I got in trouble. I tried to wash the green slime off, but it didn't go easily. As I struggled, the girls became curious. Ayshin and Zhu Zhu were about the same age, while Zhen Zhen was younger than me. She came closer, curiously sniffing the green slime.

"What are you trying to do?" she asked. "You're acting so weird. Are you in some kind of trouble?"

"Yeah, of course I'm in trouble. Don't you see I'm trying to clean off this mess?"

"Let me know if you need any help, Levend," Ayshin offered loudly, keen to yet again solve her little brother's problems.

I hated to give Ayshin another chance to act like my mother, but I had no choice. These girls were smart; even I had to admit it. They always found practical solutions to complicated problems. They got the water hose and tried to blast the slime off my body, but it didn't budge. I tried rubbing it with a cloth to get it off my skin, but that didn't work either. The slime felt like a new skin covering my body. Not that it was drying out; it was as slimy as when I'd first got it on me.

"How am I going to get rid of it?" I asked, starting to blubber.

"I have an idea!" said Ayshin. "Let's jump into the ocean, and maybe the salty sea water will wash it off."

This seemed like a great idea, so we went to the beach.

Once we arrived, we started walking into the ocean. The water got deeper, up to my knees; there was no change in the slime.

Up to my belly button; no change in the slime.

Up to my neck; no change in the slime.

It was official; the ocean water wasn't working. I found the courage to take one more step, but the slime was still there. In fact, it had expanded, swelling around my body so it looked like I was wearing a suit made of balloons! By now, I was totally submerged. The girls were swimming alongside me, but I was walking on the seabed, bubbles spilling out of my mouth.

After thirty seconds, the girls decided I was drowning. Ayshin started to panic and dove down to save me, but I gestured to her that I was okay. She couldn't hold her breath long, but I continued to walk under the sea, making bubbles. I was touching fish, collecting rocks, and all the while, the girls watched me from above in amazement. After a while, I got out of the water, screaming with joy.

At first, they couldn't believe what was going on. I barely believed it myself – it was like some kind of magic. It *had* to be magic. I felt such joy in that moment... but also a tinge of fear.

"This is… this is something special," I said. "But we can't tell anyone. Something this amazing has to be kept secret."

"But how can you keep it a secret if you can't remove it?" Ayshin asked.

Just as she finished her sentence, I sneezed, and the slimy suit ballooned into a huge bubble. It shrank back quickly, but I realized I could expand the bubble from inside by blowing through my nose. I huffed it larger and larger, and Ayshin popped it with a pin. Instantly, it curled back from the puncture like a banana skin, freeing me. I was sad to lose it, so I quickly pulled it back on. Immediately, it sealed around me like it had never been popped. Three or four more times, I blew it up and the girls popped me free. None of us had ever seen anything like it.

"I'm calling it a 'seabubble'!" I shouted triumphantly, climbing out of the now limp suit. Once I was free, we folded the seabubble and put it in my backpack.

"Secret?" I asked, but Zhu Zhu was hesitant.

"Should we talk to Mr. Alaaddin about it? Maybe it's what he's been trying to make in his factory all this time."

"I can't believe you're even suggesting we talk to that sorcerer!" said Ayshin. "He'd just take the seabubble from us. We shouldn't say anything to anyone until we know more about it. Let's come back tomorrow to see if it still works. It *seems* to repair itself, but we haven't really put it to the test."

The next morning, we snuck out of the house early and took

the seabubble with us. We met with Zhu Zhu and Zhen Zhen at the beach, and I pulled on my seabubble and walked into the ocean. It still worked!

Without hesitation, we all ran to the abandoned well near Alaaddin's rubber factory and collected the remaining slime. There was just enough to make three more seabubbles. That was fine by us: one for me, one for Ayshin, one for Zhu Zhu, and one for Zhen Zhen.

SHARK ATTACK

CHAPTER SIX

BUBBLE FISHING

As much as I wanted to keep my seabubble a secret, I also wanted to use it for fishing, and Mr. Ice was the only person I wanted to go fishing with. To be honest, I also wanted to show it off. I packed my seabubble and showed up in front of *Eyass* at five o'clock in the morning.

There were twenty other kids, all competing with their rhymes, but when it was my turn, I had a new one for him:

Mr. Ice, Mr. Ice,
come out of your Eyass.
I brought you a bubble,
let's go make some trouble.

Mr. Ice was so excited to see me that I could have been selected even without a rhyme.

"Okay, Levend," he said, "you won. You're coming fishing

with me today. Now, what's this 'bubble'? Are you going to give me some gum?"

"No," I said. "I'm not going to give you anything, for now. It's a surprise for when we arrive at our secret place."

I was so eager to show my invention to Mr. Ice!

We jumped aboard *Eyass*, and soon, we arrived at our fishing spot. We weren't so lucky that day; the fish weren't biting, and Mr. Ice wanted to move to a different place. He started to pull the anchor, but it didn't move.

"This is interesting," he said. "This has never happened to me before."

"Let me handle this, Mr. Ice," I told him.

"And just what do you intend to do, Mr. Levend?" he asked jokingly. "I'll just signal for another boat to rescue us."

"I can solve this problem," I insisted.

"Okay, show me what you can do, then," he replied.

He didn't have anything to lose, and he was intrigued by my confidence. I asked him to give me my backpack, and I pulled out my seabubble.

"What is that disgusting thing?" he asked. "It looks like a slimy ball of slugs."

"Well, this something is what I call a 'seabubble'."

"Seabubble? What's that?"

"You'll see. It's kind of amazing," I said, pulling it on. Once

I was covered, I jumped into the water without hesitation, and Mr. Ice cried out in surprise.

"Hey, I can't swim!" he shouted. "If something happens to you, I can't save you!"

"Don't worry. I'll be safe in my seabubble."

I grabbed the anchor chain and pulled on it to lower myself, the suit's segments inflating around me. In the meantime, Mr. Ice anxiously waited for me to emerge. It took almost three minutes for me to reach the bottom, but I was comfortable in the seabubble, whistling and making bubbles. I did that for Mr. Ice. As long as I was making bubbles, he would know I was alive. I didn't want him jumping in to try and save me – he might drown himself!

Down below, I touched the seabed. The anchor was stuck under a rock, which I reached out and jiggled. The anchor came free easily, and I used my seabubble to slowly rise to the surface.

Mr. Ice pulled me back into the boat. The seabubble had worked perfectly.

"I have been sailing the seas my entire life," he said, awestruck, "and I have never seen anything like this. Even a grown man can't stay underwater that long. How did you do that?"

"Seabubble!" I chortled.

"For pity's sake," he replied, "would you please explain to me what a seabubble is?"

"I think it's a kind of magical thing, really."

"Magical?"

"Yeah. I don't know exactly how it works. It's slimy and soft in the air, but it gets harder the deeper you go underwater, and you can breathe the whole time!"

"Perhaps it absorbs oxygen from the water, like a fish" said Mr. Ice, grabbing his beard. "But where did you get it? Are there more like it?"

I decided not to tell him about the other seabubbles. I'd already shared too much.

"I found it at the bottom of a well. And… no, there aren't any others. But, I'd be happy to use mine to help you."

"Thank you for the offer. You say you found it in a well?"

"Yes. An abandoned well behind Alaaddin's rubber factory."

"Hmmm. I figured that sorcerer had something to do with this seabubble."

I smiled inside when he said "sorcerer", because it confirmed what I had always believed about the strange man.

"Maybe you can ask Mr. Alaaddin to make one for you."

"I don't think it is a good idea to talk to Alaaddin about this. Let's go back to Yalova."

"Wait," I objected. I wasn't ready to go back. "I didn't come all the way out here just to save your little boat! I want to do some fishing with my seabubble."

"You know it works," said Mr. Ice. "Let's not waste more time here."

"But I really want to go fishing!"

"We can come back another time. It's getting late; we should get back to the iskele."

"C'mon, Mr. Ice! This will be so much fun! Don't make me show seabubble to some other fisherman just for the chance to use it."

"I… All right, but just for ten minutes, okay?"

Before he'd finished his sentence, I was in the water. Mr. Ice rigged some of the fishing poles with bait and lowered them into the sea. I could see how the fish were moving around the bait. All I had to do was bring the hooks next to the fish. Once they bit, Mr. Ice pulled them up to the boat. We continued to fish like this for some time.

Another fish, probably the biggest of the day, bit the bait, but I realized that Mr. Ice wasn't pulling it up to the surface. There was no way he could have failed to notice it.

I looked up at the surface. There were at least ten large fish circling the boat. But not just any fish. These were great white sharks, the most dangerous creatures in the water. Mr. Ice was trying to steer them away, throwing fish to direct their movements, but they were swallowing the fish in single bites. The sharks were nowhere near satisfied, even after Mr. Ice had thrown almost all the fish we'd caught. They wanted more, and they had no intention of leaving. Knowing he couldn't sail off and leave me alone, Mr. Ice had started to poke the sharks with a spear. Unfortunately, that just agitated them even more.

Eventually, one of the sharks saw me and dove deeper. A

moment later, I looked up to see a splash as Mr. Ice jumped into the water. He had tied a rope around his waist and was holding a knife. He waved his hands and legs frantically, swinging his knife as he fell onto the seabed behind me. Once he was upright, he pointed for me to look up. I pulled myself closer to Mr. Ice, knowing that he couldn't hold his breath for much longer. We had to face the sharks.

I signaled for him to be calm and save his energy, then I started pulling us up toward the surface. The sharks didn't waste any time; one was already barreling toward us. It came straight at me, its maw big enough to swallow me whole. Just before it bit, Mr. Ice turned sideways, pushed me aside, and stuck his wooden leg into the shark's jaws. I could hear its teeth splintering the wood, and some even came loose. The shark wasn't happy about losing some of its teeth, but it was even less pleased when Mr. Ice stabbed it. He plunged his knife so deep that it got stuck!

Even then, the shark didn't stop, turning around and launching another attack. As it rushed forward, Mr. Ice put his good hand on top of the shark's nose and leapt onto its back! He crammed his hook inside the shark's mouth and pulled it sideways, splitting open one side. The shark shook him off and passed by, leaving a trail of blood.

In an instant, all the other sharks dove down and started to circle us. Beyond them, I could see the injured shark turning around and swimming back at full speed. He was determined to get some meat! Mr. Ice didn't have much energy left, but in a last-ditch effort, he swam in front of me, sacrificing himself as a shield. The shark's jaws were about to crush him, but there was more than one shark looking for a meal. The other sharks had already smelled the blood, and they didn't care whose it was. Just before the injured shark could attack Mr. Ice, another of the beasts took a huge chunk from its side. The other sharks crowded around, and it took them just a few seconds to finish their friend off. The water turned red and I could barely see anything.

But the sharks weren't finished. They continued to circle us, and Mr. Ice was about to burst from his long-held breath. I needed to move fast and get him to the boat. In that moment, I didn't care about the sharks. Mr. Ice had saved my life. It was my turn to save his.

Ignoring the sharks was the only option, even if it didn't seem like a great one. I managed to pull us within ten meters of the surface, but one of the sharks was swimming straight for Mr. Ice, sensing his weakness. I pulled him behind me, just before the shark took a bite. He was willing to die for me like a father, now it was my turn to die for him like a son. At that moment, our lives were joined together.

The shark's teeth snapped closed on me, but they shattered. It couldn't pierce my seabubble, and it didn't like the taste of it, either. The shark released its grip and spat me out!

I was ecstatic, barely able to believe my seabubble had protected me from a shark bite. The rest of the sharks made one more circle and left. They'd given up, realizing we weren't going to be their food.

In an instant, I turned back to Mr. Ice. He had stopped breathing. I pulled him out of the water and began pressing his chest repeatedly, doing my best. Suddenly, he began to cough! He coughed and coughed, spitting up water. I'd saved him!

After a few minutes of watery coughs, he turned to look at me, his eyes squinting in the sun.

"Levend, thank you for saving my life."

"No, Mr. Ice," I replied. "Thank you. You were willing to die for me. Now, I truly know that you love me. You proved it beyond a doubt."

Mr. Ice smiled with great satisfaction. "My son…" he whispered.

He couldn't complete his sentence because he was too exhausted. Instead, he closed his eyes.

I sailed *Eyass* back to Yalova by myself, and I wasn't surprised that Mr. Ice slept all the way. The old man had been through quite an ordeal. I woke him when we arrived at the shore, and he was in good spirits. I told him that I would clean up the boat while he relaxed. He sat on a chair and watched me curiously as I cleaned the boat. He looked as if he'd never seen me before. He didn't say a word, content just to watch me.

"Mr. Ice," I said once I had finished cleaning the boat, "you threw all the fish to the sharks. There's only one mahi-mahi left. Is it okay if I take it with me?"

"Of course," he said, breaking his silence. "You can take the mahi-mahi." He paused a moment. "Do you want to go fishing with me again, one week from now?"

I wasn't surprised he'd invited me, but he seemed a little hesitant.

"Sure," I said, "I'll be here next week. Do I need to prepare a rhyme?"

"No. Just bring your seabubble. I may need your help again."

"I'll see you next time, Mr. Ice, but the seabubble must remain a secret. Can you promise not to tell anybody?"

"Of course. Your secret is safe with me."

I trusted him, of course, but something felt off. It was clear to me we had grown quite close on this day – like father and son – but his invitation definitely had something to do with the seabubble.

I slung the mahi-mahi into my fish bucket and headed home. Any other kid would have been happy to bring home a mahi-mahi, but I was used to hauling home tons of fish from an outing with Mr. Ice. It was disappointing to return with only one.

I took the long way home to think. The seabubble worked for fishing, and it was shark-proof! I'd already started to imagine how I could use my seabubble to catch fish during my next trip out.

I walked home with one mahi-mahi in my bucket, daydreaming all the way. The summer would be fun, and I was on track to make tons of money. Maybe I'd even catch the biggest and most interesting fish in town and be really popular!

AYSHIN'S LECTURE

CHAPTER SEVEN

IS FISHING A CRIME?

When I arrived home, Ayshin was waiting for me. She saw I was carrying one fish in a bucket and immediately realized something was going on.

"How come you caught only one mahi-mahi today?" she quizzed me. "Even on your worst days, you bring home more than one fish."

"I wasn't lucky," I replied, shrugging. "The fisherman I went out with wasn't good today. He wasted a lot of my time."

I wasn't lying; Mr. Ice had wasted quite a bit of time with the anchor problem. Unfortunately, she was persistent.

"I see you're also carrying a backpack. You never take your backpack when you go fishing."

She knew I'd taken the seabubble, but I still tried to dodge the question.

"Oh, the backpack was for snacks."

"What was for lunch?" she asked. She could be really annoying sometimes. "Who prepared it? What happened to your regular lunchbox?"

It was clear she wasn't going to stop, so I spilled the beans.

"Okay, okay," I said, "I'll fess up. I took the seabubble with me."

"I knew you'd do that! I thought we promised each other that we'd keep the seabubble our secret. Just three days, and you already showed it to somebody. Shame on you!"

"But I wanted to see how we could use it to catch fish!" I tried to explain, but Ayshin was furious.

"Shame on you! How could you break your promise? Do you know what could happen if people learned about the seabubble? What if bad people became aware of seabubbles? They might do *anything* to have one. You put our lives in danger!"

I was out of words. I'd never thought about bad people wanting to get the seabubbles; I'd only thought about using them for fishing. Sadly, my sister was right. The seabubbles *could* be weapons. The gravity of owning one hit me at that point. It was entirely possible that gangsters, Jynx pirates, or even King Korsan's spies would be after us.

In the meantime, Ayshin was enough to deal with on her own. I was suddenly so distraught that I didn't even hear her anymore, but she grabbed my shirt and started shaking me.

"How many times am I going to ask you? Answer me! Which fisherman did you go with?"

"Nobody!" I said.

She pushed me down to the ground. "You liar! You put my life, your life, and the lives of everybody you know in danger. Now, you're telling me you went fishing with nobody?"

A few minutes ago, I had been the happiest kid in the world. Now, I was the most scared kid in the world. Before I realized it, Ayshin was on top of me. She was smaller than me, but she had heavy hands. When she punched, it hurt. She kept shouting.

"Who did you go fishing with? Tell me the truth!" Tears began to pour from her eyes. "How could you do this? How?"

"It was Mr. Ixbrrse…" I whispered.

"What are you saying? Speak clearly! Who did you go with?"

"You're choking me!"

She stepped back and took a deep breath.

"Okay. I'm calm now. Tell me who you went fishing with. I promise I won't hurt you. We'll find a solution to this problem. I promise. I'm your older sister, and I'll protect you."

"It was… Mr. Ice," I said, blurting out the name that she least wanted to hear.

She punched me on the shoulder.

"Of all the fishermen at the iskele, you chose to show our seabubble to by far the wackiest person in the town! Are you kidding me?" I began trying to defend Mr. Ice, but she wasn't in the mood to listen. "He's a psycho. He never talks to anybody! He's definitely a pirate. Are you kidding me? He'll want

71

to take the seabubble for himself! Why did you show it to him? Why?"

I covered my face with my hands, mumbling, "Can you calm down, please? I know I've done a terrible thing, but I thought you were going to help me... I mean help *us*. I am very, very, very sorry."

She opened her mouth as if to continue shouting, then closed it and took a deep breath. We both calmed down, and she gave me a big hug.

"It's okay, my GeGe. We're in this together, I promise you, I'll never yell at you again. Let's start from the beginning. Tell me what you've told Mr. Ice."

I told her everything that had happened while fishing, skipping only the part where Mr. Ice had called me his son and how I felt about him in return. Ayshin listened carefully, then, after a moment of quiet contemplation, spoke.

"I'm going to call Zhu Zhu and Zhen Zhen. We have to tell them what's going on. Their lives are in danger, as well. They have to know about this, then we'll decide together what to do."

A few hours later, Zhu Zhu and Zhen Zhen joined us. Ayshin told them what had happened, and they talked among themselves for a while. Finally, Zhu Zhu spoke to me, with a calm voice, thankfully.

"Levend, there are a few good signs and a few bad signs. The worst sign is that he invited you again and asked you to bring your seabubble. He was definitely interested in the seabubble, and whatever he's planning, it appears it will take him a week to get ready. Because of that, I don't think he's going to mention the seabubble to anybody. He'll want to keep it to himself. The good news is that we only need to deal with him, but the better news is that you told him we only have one seabubble. So he isn't going to bring a bunch of pirates here hunting for seabubbles. Our family and friends won't be dragged into this." She took a deep breath. "There's only one thing we can do."

"What?" I asked.

"Tomorrow morning, we will go directly to the militia and have him arrested."

"What are we going to tell the militia?" I asked, hating the idea. "He hasn't committed any crime. The worst thing he did was be unfriendly with the other fishermen. He took almost all the kids in town fishing and brought each and every one of them back safely. They all seemed to enjoy it!" Probably for the first time in my life, I was actually making sense, and the girls were puzzled. "I don't want to give up my seabubble. But as soon as we tell the police that we have one, they'll take it from us. I think we should wait. I don't think Mr. Ice is going to do anything bad to us. He's actually a really nice man."

"I don't know about that part, but you're right about the rest," Ayshin said, calming down again. "Let's wait a few days. We have to develop a plan to handle him ourselves. At worst, we'll just give him your seabubble and he should leave us alone. But promise me you won't go fishing with that ugly pirate again. All right?"

"Yes," I replied reluctantly, but I crossed my fingers behind my back. What she was saying made sense, but I trusted Mr. Ice. He wasn't going to harm me.

I turned my head and noticed that Zhen Zhen was behind me. She had seen me cross my fingers. I shot her a dark look. She didn't say anything then, but I knew that eventually she'd tell Ayshin not to trust me.

LITTLE FAN FAN AND GIANT YANG YANG

CHAPTER EIGHT

WHO IS MR. BEN ICE ?

Once I got a taste of going fishing with the seabubble, there was no going back. I waited anxiously to go fishing with Mr. Ice again. I even went to the iskele to look for him in the days that followed, but he was nowhere to be found. He disappeared for the whole week, not even touching *Eyass*. I wondered where he'd gone, thinking that perhaps the fight with the sharks had injured him.

Finally, the fishing day arrived. I woke up early and put the seabubble in my backpack, sneaking out before Ayshin woke. My seabubble would make fishing a breeze, and Mr. Ice and I would be done in a couple of hours. I could be back for lunch before anybody even realized I'd left the house! I headed to the iskele, but just before I got there, I heard a familiar voice.

"Levend, where are you going this early in the morning?"

I turned around. Sure enough, Zhu Zhu was smiling at me suspiciously. I couldn't believe my bad luck; she would surely tell Ayshin.

"Why are you running? What's in your backpack?" she asked, approaching me.

"I'm just taking my backpack to a friend. He's going fishing."

"Stop lying, Levend," she said, suddenly changing her tune. "We should never have trusted you! Zhen Zhen saw you cross your fingers when you gave your promise. We've been taking turns waiting for you here. Sure enough, you showed up. We aren't going to let you sail out with that crazy fisherman."

"Too bad," I said, stretching the words coolly. "I'm going anyway. You girls can't stop me."

"You're not going anywhere, mister! Ayshin and Zhen Zhen are on their way here, and we're going to take that seabubble away from you."

There wasn't much I could do except run to the iskele as fast as possible, so I ran. Sure enough, Mr. Ice was waiting for me. He'd packed more than the usual amount of supplies in the boat.

"Let's go, Mr. Ice," I shouted. "And fast!"

"Calm down, little boy. What's the hurry?"

"Um, I don't want to miss any morning light. This is the best time to fish, right?"

I looked at the beach. Ayshin and Zhen Zhen were running

down the hill at full speed. Scissors glinted in their hands. They were planning to cut my seabubble to shreds!

"Let's *go*," I said, helping Mr. Ice untie the mooring lines.

"Okay, okay, we're leaving."

Finally, we started to move. When the girls arrived, we were already heading out to sea. They started to wave and yell at us, catching Mr. Ice's attention.

"Do you know those girls? I think they're waving at us."

"Must be my fans. Girls are crazy about me."

"Yeah, right," he chuckled. Luckily, he didn't have any interest in talking to other kids.

When we got to the deep water, Mr. Ice became serious. He started to sharpen his blades and his hook.

"Are you cutting your fingernails, Mr. Ice?" I asked, hoping to break the tension.

"Ha, ha, you're really funny," he said blankly. "Shut up before I break my leg over your head."

"Break *another* leg Mr. Ice," I said, noticing that he was wearing a brand new wooden leg. "Maybe this one will bring you luck. You should have gotten yourself a pink leg, this time!"

We chuckled then continued to sail. He was going in the opposite direction to our usual fishing grounds, and I gave him a confused look.

"We're going to catch swordfish today," he said. "Enough of the same old fish."

He told me to hold onto the captain's wheel and keep *Eyass* in the starboard direction. Orders given, he went into the captain's cabin to take a nap.

Two hours later, he emerged. Toy was sitting on his shoulder. He'd never brought his parrot fishing before, and I found the change interesting, even if he was being a little grumpy at the same time.

"We aren't going fast enough," he barked. "We should be there by now. Continue in the same direction. I'm going inside to prepare the bait and hooks."

"No problem, Mr. Ice. I can handle this."

A few hours later, I was still at the wheel, and I thought I heard a whisper.

"Beniii…"

It must be the wind, I thought to myself. A few minutes later, I heard the whisper again.

"Benice…"

Mr. Ice was inside the captain's cabin, trying to catch Toy with a fishing net. I heard it again, but this time it was louder and clearer.

"Benice, Benice, Benice! I love you."

It was Toy. Mr. Ice had said the parrot didn't speak, but she kept repeating "Benice." Eventually, Mr. Ice caught the bird and struggled to wrap a rubber band around its beak. I walked into the cabin.

"Why is Toy saying 'Benice'? What does that mean?"

He stopped trying to muzzle her but said nothing. In the meantime, Toy continued to talk.

"Benice, Benice, Benice! I love you!"

"C'mon, Mr. Ice," I said, "don't keep secrets from me. Who is Benice?"

He took a deep breath. "Okay, I'll tell you one of my biggest secrets. Benice was my lovely wife. We married when we were very young. She loved me, even though I had only one eye, one hand, and one leg. Everybody else made fun of me, but she took care of me, and I loved her from the bottom of my heart. But before she gave birth to our only son, she got very sick. I had to leave her behind to find medicine for her disease. Sadly, I was not successful in my mission."

"Did she pass away?" I asked. He didn't answer.

Instead, in a serious voice, he said, "That was in the past. Now, turn around."

"Why?" I asked.

"Turn around, I said!"

I turned around, and I was shocked to see that we were next to a huge ship.

"Where did *that* come from?" I asked. I looked up and saw men running up and down the deck. They were waving at us. I couldn't tell if they were friend or foe.

The flag on top of the ship caught my eye. It was a Jolly Roger.

I turned to Mr. Ice, only to discover he was grinning nastily. I started to put the pieces together.

Mr. Ben,

Mr. Ice,

Mr. Ben Ice,

Benice.

"Your last name isn't 'Ice', is it?" I yelled at him. "You lied to me! You made it up to sound like your wife's name."

I could already smell the ship's stench, but as we drew closer, I began to hear its crew calling out to us.

"Hey, old pirate!" yelled a Jynx man aboard the ship. "How are you doing?"

"It's so cute you named your little boat after a baby falcon," yelled another.

"Hey, BarbaRossa, old man," shouted a third. "Sewer rats still haven't gotten to your wooden leg?"

"You're the infamous Captain BarbaRossa!" I shouted. "Your secret is out!" I couldn't contain myself. "All this time, you were lying to me! You told me that you loved me like your son, liar. *Liar!* You betrayed me!"

"You're right; I am Captain BarbaRossa. After I retired, I moved to Yalova. I guess I was lucky, running into you. Now, I can get back what the seas took from me."

"What are you talking about?" I asked. "Haven't you already tortured a teenage boy enough? What do you want me for?"

"Levend," he laughed, "I don't want *you*. I want something you have."

"I hate you! Do you hear me? I hate you! You won't get anything from me."

As I shouted my defiance, one of the pirates jumped to *Eyass*. In a flash, he tied a rope around me and whisked me up to the big ship. BarbaRossa followed, the sound of cheering and chanting ringing in my ears.

"Hip, hip, hooray!

Hip, hip, hooray!

Captain BarbaRossa is back!

We'll rule the oceans again!

Hip, hip, hooray!"

A huge, bulky pirate approached us. He was a shirtless Jynx with a large B-shaped scar on the back of his shoulder. I guessed he had dressed this way to intimidate people. From the way the others acted around him, he seemed to be the captain. He strode up to BarbaRossa.

"Welcome back to the *Falcon's Blood*, BarbaRossa. It's been a long time since I saw your mangled face."

"Nice to see you too, Zamora," BarbaRossa replied. "You haven't changed a bit. You were ugly then, and you're ugly now."

Aha! This was the famous Zamora who had given BarbaRossa the picture. It seemed he hadn't been lying about his hatred for the man. They didn't shake hands, just stared at each other for a few seconds, sizing each other up.

"You are no longer the captain here," said Zamora.

"I am here to claim my ship," BarbaRossa replied. "I need the *Falcon's Blood*. You can either accept that or you can fight me. Choose the former and there's a reward in it for you."

Everybody on the deck was watching with bated breath. It was clear that most of them wanted BarbaRossa as their captain, and Zamora could only keep his position if he fought for it. The grumbling around me suggested that might not be the end of it, though. In a fair fight, Zamora could easily kill BarbaRossa. While old BarbaRossa had been getting rusty in his fishing boat, Zamora must have been flexing his muscles on the high seas. Still, that meant nothing if his victory provoked a mutiny.

Neither man was in a good position, and they were both playing their cards carefully.

"Are you offering to scratch my back, BarbaRossa? You'd have to be careful with that hook." Zamora stepped toward BarbaRossa, wrapping him in a huge bear hug. "I'm glad you're back. As long as you're on this ship, I will be your loyal servant. Take the captain's mantle."

Zamora wasn't stupid, and he'd taken the only path that seemed to guarantee he would one day be the captain again. I wondered how much of that could be due to his curiosity about what BarbaRossa was up to, and what reward it might bring.

BarbaRossa took the mantle from Zamora. He hooked the handle and lifted it high into the air.

"Once a pirate, always a pirate," he growled, holding both of his arms high. He cut a cross on his left arm with his hook, then put his lips around the bleeding scar and tasted his own blood. "My veins still bleed falcon's blood! Will you die for me?"

"*Yes!*" screamed the crew.

"Who is your captain?"

"BarbaRossa!"

"Who is going to give you back the Zanzibar Treasure?"

"BarbaRossa!"

This treasure! That had to be BarbaRossa's reason for returning to the *Falcon's Blood*. Pirates were famous for collecting treasure and hiding it for the future, since keeping too much treasure on a ship always meant trouble. I hated BarbaRossa even more. He didn't have any special feelings toward me; he was just using me to get the treasure.

The pirates rushed to welcome BarbaRossa, sticking out their hands in greeting. Zamora and his loyal crew members, mostly Jynx, merely offered forced smiles. They clearly resented BarbaRossa, but for now, there was nothing they could do but obey. They'd have to wait for the right opportunity if they wanted to get rid of him.

"My captain!" cried one Nevar crewmate.

"Is that my best friend Abdi?" roared BarbaRossa. "I see the devil still cares for his own!"

"I take care of myself," Abdi replied, "like any pirate worth his salt."

"Thank you for accepting me back and pledging your allegiance, Zamora," said BarbaRossa, the flow of blood from his cut receding. "I always treated you well, as long as you obeyed me, and you can expect the same from this point onward. It looks like you took good care of the *Falcon's Blood*, while I was away. Let's get down to business!"

"We're excited that you contacted us after all these years, BarbaRossa," Zamora added. "Can you really recover the Zanzibar Treasure this time?"

"There will be time to discuss that. I will explain in the captain's quarters." Then he turned to me. "First things first; take this useless little boy's backpack and kill him. We don't need another mouth to feed."

My heart was pounding; I had to think fast and find a way to escape. I understood now that once he had learned about my seabubble, that was all he'd cared about.

Zamora came after me with two of his men. They held my arms and legs, pinning my head against the railings of the ship. Zamora lifted his sword.

"I suppose I'll be wearing your seabubble, after all," crowed BarbaRossa.

"Stop, stop, stop!" I screamed. "Let me speak for one second. It won't work for you!"

"Wait!" cried BarbaRossa, grabbing Zamora's arm. "What do you mean?"

"My seabubble won't fit any of your pirates. You're all too big and fat for it, and if you try to cut or tear it, you'll destroy it. If you want to use the seabubble, you'll need me, otherwise it's useless!"

All the pirates were confused. What was this "seabubble"? What was the little boy babbling about?

Zamora interrupted. "We have small pirates on this ship. They can try to fit in this seabubble."

BarbaRossa paused.

"I forgot about those little Jynxes," he mumbled. "Zamora, if you didn't kill Little Fan Fan in my absence, bring him here. He should still be the smallest pirate on this ship. I expect Giant Yang Yang will be by his side, as always."

A pirate went below deck to bring the crewmates up, leaving me to wonder what these little and giant pirates looked like. A couple of minutes later, two Jynx pirates emerged from the doorway. I was expecting to see one big and one small, but they were exactly the same size. They looked like twins, except for the fact that their mustaches were different shapes. Compared to the other pirates, they were indeed small. I couldn't tell if they were dwarfs or boys my age. BarbaRossa seemed confused as well.

"When I left the *Falcon's Blood*, Little Fan Fan was small and Giant Yang Yang was big. What happened here?"

"Well," chuckled Zamora, "after you left, Little Fan Fan ate a lot, and Giant Yang Yang ate a little. Now, they're the same size."

"Go stand next to the new boy," BarbaRossa ordered, ignoring Zamora's smart comment. They sidled up next to me, as filthy and stinky as the rest of them. Now, I could clearly see that they were boys about my age. I wondered how they could grow mustaches at such a young age. But, mustaches or not, I had been right; both Little Fan Fan and Giant Yang Yang were taller and heavier than me. I was relieved.

"There's no way my seabubble would fit these pirates," I said. "You'll need me for whatever you're trying to do."

"I can see that," growled BarbaRossa. He didn't look happy. "Zamora fed these kids too well."

Feeling somewhat safer, I couldn't resist making fun of the boys.

"You guys look about the same size," I said with a smirk on my face, "so I guess Little Fan Fan must have the 'small' brain, and Giant Yang Yang must have the 'big' brain. So, which one of you is the stupid one?"

The boy standing next to me lifted his right fist.

"Do you see this?" he asked.

"Yes," I replied. "I can see your little fist."

"This is called 'Little One'," he continued, and then he punched me in the stomach. I immediately curled up. He lifted his left fist. "Do you see this? This is Little One's brother. He's called 'Giant One'."

Bam! He punched me in the nose, and I fell flat on the deck.

"Welcome to the *Falcon's Blood*, landlubber," said his friend.

"Stop fooling around," barked BarbaRossa. "We need this boy alive, at least for several days." He turned to Little Fan Fan and Giant Yang Yang. "Now, listen to me carefully. If this boy is killed by anybody but you, I will throw both of you off the ship. If you kill this boy before I give you permission, I will throw both of you off the ship. You are responsible for keeping him alive. I will tell you when I'm done with him. Then, you can do whatever you want. Understood?"

"Heh heh, did you hear that?" whispered one of the boys. "You belong to *us* now."

"Put him in the dungeon, between Zhan Yaga and Jamie Yaga's cells," BarbaRossa continued. "Make sure he doesn't starve to death before I'm finished with him. After you put him in the dungeon, come upstairs. I want to find out how you grew those mustaches; they're better than mine!"

This entire production had left the pirates confused. Why had being small saved my life? I could see that Zamora had a lot of questions for BarbaRossa, but he was waiting until they were in the captain's quarters.

"Hey, one more thing," BarbaRossa said, pointing to Little Fan Fan. "Make sure that landlubber doesn't bother Guru. He still lives in the dungeon, right?"

"Yes, sir," replied Little Fan Fan, "he's still in there."

"Good. Tell Guru I'll visit him tonight. I need to brief him about this situation. Now, get back to work! Abdi, you come with me. We have a lot to catch up on."

Little Fan Fan and Giant Yang Yang dragged me down into the dark dungeon, yammering away to each other.

"Why is everybody so curious about our mustaches?"

"I think they're jealous."

Although my stomach risked meeting the little and giant fists again, I couldn't resist.

"C'mon, guys. Have you ever seen a young boy with a mustache? Get real."

"Really, kids don't get mustaches?" asked one. "When *do* people get mustaches, then?"

It sounded as if they'd never met another kid. Could I be the first kid they'd met? If so, it didn't buy me any special treatment, and they shoved me into the dungeon without a care, not even bothering to lock the door.

"You stay here. Don't think about moving; we'd find you and you'd meet my fists again. And also, a word of advice: stay away from the witches."

"You mean Zhan Yaga and Jamie Yaga?" I asked. "What do they look like? Are they friendly?"

"Oh, don't worry, they'll find you. Then you'll see."

"Hey," one asked the other, "he doesn't have a mustache;

are you sure Zhan Yaga isn't going to harm him? I don't want BarbaRossa to punish us if she kills him."

"She hasn't killed anybody yet."

"But Jamie Yaga certainly might! She bit a rat once!"

"Nah, don't worry about the Yagas. They'll just be walking around, shaking and swaying their hips as usual. I don't think they're going to bother him."

"Not much we can do about it, I suppose. After all, BarbaRossa *told* us to put him in a cell between the Yagas. Let's go."

"Hey, boys," I cried, unable to hold it in any longer. "Don't leave me alone with the Yagas, please! BarbaRossa will be very upset if I die. And who is this Guru? Is he dangerous?"

"Don't worry," Little Fan Fan called back, already walking away. "We'll return tomorrow. Too bad you don't have a mustache. It might protect you from Zhan Yaga."

"And good luck with Guru," Giant Yang Yang called back. "He's at least as dangerous as the Yagas!"

"This isn't a dungeon. It's more like a zoo!" I cried in despair.

They left, and I was alone in the dark. I could hear only the rhythm of waves beating against the ship, but I could feel Zhan Yaga and Jamie Yaga pacing around the dungeon, shaking and swaying their hips as if dancing.

I curled up in the corner of my cell. Those stupid twins! They hadn't even bothered to lock the door. That would have at least protected me from the Yagas.

MAGICAL NIGHT AT FALCON HEART'S RATLINES

CHAPTER NINE

CAN WE BECOME FRIENDS ?

My first night in the dungeon was horrible. I fought with cockroaches and mice all night long. In the middle of the night, BarbaRossa and Abdi came down. They didn't bother to visit me, but sat in another cell and talked to somebody for hours. I assumed it was Guru. They started out laughing, but their talk became serious and then, eventually, heated. Just as I was nodding off, a cell door slammed open and someone charged out into the corridor.

"Just tell me straight!" said a voice I didn't recognize.

"It isn't that simple, Guru," said BarbaRossa, following him out of the cell.

I could hear them clearly now, but I still didn't know what they were talking about.

"It's simpler than you're making it," replied Guru. "Tell me why."

There was a moment of silence.

"Abdi," said BarbaRossa, "go up to the deck and make sure no one is eavesdropping."

"Yes, Captain," said Abdi, and I heard his boots on the wooden stairs. There was more silence, then BarbaRossa began to speak in a much quieter voice.

"I understand your frustration," he said, "but now is not the time to express it."

"Who knows when you'll return again?" Guru replied, also whispering. "You swore to teach me, to pass on your wisdom."

"And I did!" said BarbaRossa.

"You taught me a lot," agreed Guru. "You taught me how to be brave, and thoughtful, and sly, and courageous, and cunning, and forthright. You taught me all the ways I could approach a situation to win the day, but you never taught me which was best. You promised you would tell me how to live, how to *be*. You promised not just the tools of life, but a deeper understanding of how and why to use them. When a man challenges me to a fight, I know I can beat him one-on-one, or I can trick him into giving up, or I can inspire others to fight for me, but I never know which is the best option! Teach me that and I'll thank you."

"It's not that simple," BarbaRossa replied.

"Yes it is!" shouted Guru. "Give me a direction and I'll stay true to it. Should I be cruel or should I be merciful? Should I be strong or should I be smart? Should I rule others like a king or care for them like a priest? Tell me how to *be!*"

"I will," BarbaRossa said, clearly exhausted, "but not now. You have more potential than anyone I've ever known, but you *must* conceal it until you have learned your way. I know, I know, I should *tell* you your way. I thought I had lost the right, but now… Yes, I can tell you. Yes, I *will* tell you, but not on this ship, where the walls have ears and any man might slit your throat for an advantage. If it's with my dying breath, I will tell you what you want to know. Is that enough? Will you trust me?"

I don't know what Guru replied, he must have either shaken his head or nodded, but then there was the sound of footsteps and his cell door closed again. BarbaRossa stood in the hallway for a few minutes, but he didn't say anything to me, and after a little while, he was gone, too.

After he left, I couldn't sleep. I was too alert, expecting a visit from Zhan Yaga and Jamie Yaga, but they never came.

The next morning, Little Fan Fan and Giant Yang Yang came to see me. I was strangely relieved.

"Did they visit you?"

"Who?"

"The Yagas, you stupid!"

"No," I said. "Neither of them came."

"Well, you're a lucky boy, then. Don't worry, they'll show up eventually."

"You know, I don't care if the Yagas show up." I kind of did, actually.

Little Fan Fan laughed.

"Why would you? We were only messing with you. Actually, those lady Yagas are harmless. They run around the ship all the time. They're clueless. At night, they sleep in huge eggs! They should be awake now; we'll show you how harmless they are."

"Hey, Guru," called Giant Yang Yang. "Why don't you join us? It's okay to stop reading books for a while."

"He's a good guy, but he doesn't mingle with us much," Giant Yang Yang told me. "He thinks he has more important things to worry about. Let's see if he's going to come out of his cell this time."

Guru did come out. I was expecting a Jynx but was surprised to see he was a Nevar. Piracy was rare for them, as King Korsan was usually generous with his fellow Nevars. He looked a few years older than us, and he was holding a clarinet. The twins started to hum a melody, and he played along with a haunting harmony.

I heard one of the Yagas start to shake her hips to the rhythm of the song; she moved down the stairs and toward the door of the dungeon. She looked like some kind of psychedelic witch. She shuffled her feet but appeared to be floating, and she came close enough to look me in the eye. Then, she started to wave her hands in a circular motion.

"Which one is this?" I asked.

"This is Jamie Yaga. Isn't she nice? She's the best entertainment we have on the ship."

"You guys have a really high standard for entertainment," I grumbled. "You should join a circus and tour the empire."

"Do you really think so?" asked Little Fan Fan.

"Never mind," I sighed.

Jamie Yaga continued shaking her hips, the beads of her skirt clicking musically, and I started to clap my hands to the rhythm. Just a few minutes later, Zhan Yaga came down as well, and both Yagas started to dance around me. Before I realized what I was doing, I was shaking my hips. I realized they had psychic powers and were probably controlling my mind, but I didn't care; I was actually having fun.

While everyone danced, Guru took a break from playing music and leaned closer to me.

"You must find a way to make the captain guarantee your safety with the pirate oath," he said. "If you can do that, no one will be able to kill you."

"Yeah, I'm sure pirates keep all their promises," I said sarcastically. Guru looked ready to say more, but Little Fan Fan shouted for him to keep playing, and so he did.

Eventually, we all got tired. Zhan and Jamie Yaga went

to their cells, and the boys went to the deck to do their chores.

As we continued our journey to Zanzibar, I started to develop a bond with Little Fan Fan and Giant Yang Yang. They visited me in the dungeon regularly. They tried to look tough, but underneath it, they were eager to talk to me. One day, they brought my meal as usual and didn't leave. I sensed they wanted to hang out with me instead of going back to the deck.

"How old are you guys?" I asked, hoping to initiate a conversation. "I'm fourteen."

"We're fourteen, too."

"What's it like to be a pirate? I envy you a little bit. You're living such an exotic life, jumping from one adventure to another."

"It's not as much fun as you think, Levend."

"Why not?"

"We got used to living without any other kids around, more or less, but we kind of miss our parents. We never met them, you see; we came to this ship when we were babies."

"Really? I thought one of the Yagas was your mother."

"What? Why? No, that's not true. Do we look *that* weird?"

I was going to say, *Yes, it's hard to be any weirder than those dancing Yagas, but you're awfully close. You can't find a mustache on many kids*, but I held my tongue.

"Zhan Yaga is Zamora's wife," Little Fan Fan explained. "We heard rumors that Zamora found her running around the

Qingdao Forests. They fell in love at first sight, and Zamora brought her to the *Falcon's Blood*. He's not a good man, but he truly loves her. See how happy she is? They make a nice couple."

"So, what's Jamie's story?"

"She's Zamora's mother; I don't know how she came to the ship, but I heard a rumor that Jamie Yaga hatched out of a big, purple egg. She was already here when we got on the ship."

"How did *you* come to the *Falcon's Blood*?"

"Somebody brought us to this ship when we were babies. They don't talk about it, but we think Zamora had something to do with it."

"Wait a minute," I said, trying to understand what was going on. "You grew up here?"

"That's right," Giant Yang Yang responded. "If you don't count pirate raids, we've only left the ship once in our lives, though we were lucky enough to meet another kid."

I was shocked to hear that the twins had never met their parents. On top of that, they'd only ever met one other kid!

"How did you get all this information?" I asked. "What do you know about BarbaRossa, how did he become a pirate?"

"BarbaRossa is the greatest pirate captain who ever lived. He's the true master of the seas. His maritime skills made us rich, and he brought us home safely from many dangerous adventures. His entire crew – Orhuns, Jynxes, and Nevars – all love him, not just because of his skills, but because of how he treats us. He's always fair and respectful."

"What about Zamora and his men? They didn't seem so happy."

"That's true. Zamora has many reasons to dislike BarbaRossa and always wanted to overthrow him. That's probably why BarbaRossa only trusts Guru to run the *Falcon's Blood*. Well, he might trust Abdi, but he'd never want the responsibility."

"Really, he only trusts Guru? I thought Nevars didn't like the high seas. Also, isn't he too young to be trusted to run a pirate ship?"

"Once you get to know Guru, you'll find out why. I think BarbaRossa is training him to be a captain. He shares all of his knowledge with him. Guru doesn't mingle with any of the crew. He's a bit stuck up, but he told us how BarbaRossa became a pirate."

"I'd like to hear BarbaRossa's story," I said. "I can't understand what drives that man. He was nice to me when we were in Yalova, but now he's dragged me to a pirate ship."

"BarbaRossa's story is very complicated. Can we talk about it later?"

Apparently, Little Fan Fan didn't want to waste his time with me talking about BarbaRossa. After a moment of silence, Little Fan Fan could no longer resist asking the big question.

"Can we become friends? What do you say?"

"Sure," I said, giving them a warm smile. "I'd be happy to be your friend, but I'm not entirely sure you even know what friendship means."

"That's heartbreaking! Why would you say such a thing?" replied Little Fan Fan. My answer really took the wind out of him.

"I'm sorry, guys. I didn't mean to insult you. It's just that you can't ask for true friendship, because it's not something anyone can just give. It grows over time. You share experiences, you play together, you help each other through the hard times. Then, one day, you're looking back on those memories and you realize you have it and that you wouldn't trade it for anything."

"We never thought about it that way," said Little Fan Fan. "What do we need to do?"

"Nothing! Just be yourselves. All we have to do is play, talk, and have fun together. Today was a very good day to start our friendship; I hope it lasts for the rest of our lives. But true friendship is very, very, very hard to find. Only a few lucky people in the whole world have true friendship. Maybe we'll be some of those lucky kids. But, guys, since we're starting our friendship, can I ask you a favor? I want to make sure we start on a good note, otherwise we can kiss our friendship goodbye."

"Anything you want, Levend. I'm sure we can sort it out."

"Can you promise not to kill me? You normally don't want to

be friends with your potential killers. But I want a friendship's promise, not any of this pirate oath nonsense I've heard about."

"Sure. We give you a friendship's promise that we won't kill you."

It was a good start, and it came as a relief, since I was as curious about them as they were about me.

"What kinds of games do you play here? I'd guess you don't play any ball games or games that require teams, 'cause there are no other kids to play with you."

"You're right."

"What do you do, then?"

"We're kind of good at peeling potatoes in the kitchen," Little Fan Fan said with a shrug.

"I'm not sure what kind of game that is," I said, "but I'll pass, thanks. What else can we play?"

"We're good at cleaning the deck. How about playing a 'cleaning the deck' game?"

"Nope," I replied. "I'll pass on cleaning the deck as well. What else do you have? Chess?"

"That sounds like a landlubber's game. How about swords?"

"That's a little bit too rough for a landlubber."

"How about 'rat lines' game?"

"That sounds interesting. What's a rat line?"

"You saw all the ropes going to the mast and sails? They're

called rat lines. Fat pirates can't climb the rat lines, but we can do it really fast. It's our specialty!"

"How fast can you guys go?"

"Really fast!"

"Can you show me?"

"Yeah! Tonight, right after midnight, we'll come get you."

"Cool. I look forward to it."

There was no wind in the air that night. Little Fan Fan and Giant Yang Yang came down and took me and Guru to the rat lines. It turned out they were very, very fast climbers. By the time I managed to get a good grip and start climbing, they were already at the top! We went up and down the rat lines all night.

At the end of the night, we sat at the top of the mast to count the shooting stars. Guru was the winner that night; he counted thirty-two, and I only counted twenty-nine.

Exhausted, all four of us fell asleep on the mast. Our friendship was born that night.

LOBSTER-POPSTER CHASING LEVEND

CHAPTER TEN

TREASURE HUNT

iant Yang Yang woke me up from my comfortable sleep on top of the mast. "We've arrived in Zanzibar, landlubber. It's time to reveal why BarbaRossa dragged you all the way here."

I looked down from the mast, spotting commotion on the deck. Pirates were lowering the sails and dropping anchor. Guru was already gone from the mast, and Little Fan Fan was carefully observing the deck.

"Let's get down before the old man finds out we spent the night outside the dungeon," Giant Yang Yang instructed. "We need to be on deck as soon as possible."

"I thought you were going to tell me more about BarbaRossa," I protested.

"There's no time for chit-chat. You'll find out more about BarbaRossa after you finish the job you came here to do."

We climbed down and proceeded to the deck, lining up in front of BarbaRossa. He threw the seabubble to me.

"Put this on," he ordered. "It's time to work."

"What exactly am I supposed to do?" I asked.

"Years ago, we lost our mother ship, the *Falcon's Heart*. I was a very young pirate at that time, and it was my first journey aboard a pirate ship. The *Falcon's Heart* was carrying treasure we'd pillaged from Zanzibar. Unfortunately, before we took our treasure, the *Falcon's Heart* sank to the bottom of the sea, along with our captain, Jamoka."

"I remember that day so clearly," Zamora added. "We were so young. After my father Jamoka sank with the other ship, I was supposed to become the captain of the *Falcon's Blood*. I had barely begun to grieve when you challenged me and took the mantle."

Anybody could tell Zamora still resented the loss, but even I knew it was the pirate way. If you didn't rise to a challenge, you lost.

Zamora continued, "We made a fortune by sinking ships, pillaging villages, and killing innocent people. Eventually, we became the most fearsome pirate gang the world had ever seen. Only the Zanzibar Treasure eluded us. We've come back to recover the Zanzibar Treasure so many times, but we couldn't retrieve it. The shipwreck was just too deep and the waters too treacherous."

These guys sink ships and kill people for fun! That is disgusting! How low can they get? If I'd been in any doubt, I knew now that these pirates were barbarians and had no respect for life. I had to find a way to save my own.

"Stop dwelling on the past, Zamora. Let's focus on the present and the job at hand. We are going to get that treasure this time," said BarbaRossa. He focused his attention to me. "Now, little boy, listen to me. You're going to put your seabubble on and bring that treasure back to me. Understood?"

"What if I can't bring it back?"

"Well, then, I guess either Little Fan Fan or Giant Yang Yang will have to kill you. Take your pick."

I was in deep trouble, and I scrambled to find a way out of my situation.

"But if I bring the treasure back, you won't need me after that, either! You'll still have one of your goons kill me." I decided to follow Guru's advice. "I demand you give me the pirate oath to spare my life after we recover the treasure."

"You're a smart kid, Levend," said BarbaRossa, "but why should I give you the pirate oath?"

"I'm not going into the water unless you give me your word. And this pirate oath better not be a joke," I replied.

The pirate crew were clearly surprised by the way I was talking to BarbaRossa. Talking back to the captain wasn't tolerated on a pirate ship, usually resulting in someone ending up in a dungeon or walking the plank, but my response seemed to have rattled him. Thankfully, he kept his cool; the Zanzibar Treasure was clearly important to him.

"The pirate oath is a pirate's honor. We may kill people for fun, but when a pirate makes a promise, he will keep it to eternity. I promise now that if you bring me the treasure, I will spare your life."

"I accept your promise," I shouted, then I turned to Zamora and his men. "But how can you stop all these other ugly pirates from killing me?"

Zamora stared daggers.

"When a captain makes a promise," said BarbaRossa, "that applies to everybody on the ship."

"Okay," I said. "We're getting somewhere, then. I have one more question."

"The pirate oath is sacred to all pirates," he barked. He was growing impatient, but I didn't care; I had to save myself. "You may ask your question, but this is the last one, and don't even dare make a joke of it."

"What happens if you die and there's a new captain?" I asked, looking at Zamora. "Would the new captain honor the previous captain's oath?"

Zamora's glare subsided, and I could tell he was trying not to chuckle. BarbaRossa, on the other hand, was less pleased.

"Maybe I should forget about giving you the pirate oath and kill you right now." He swore to himself. "Okay. The captain gives the pirate oath on behalf of the ship, and with the ship it stays. Once the oath is given, all who sail aboard the *Falcon's Blood* will obey it to eternity, regardless of who is the captain."

"All right, then," I said, pleased to have upset my captor. "Since I have your pirate oath, and everybody here as my witness, I will help you." I was happy to have turned the tables and shown up BarbaRossa a little, but it didn't change the fact that I had to do as he said. "Tell me what to do now."

"Come to the captain's cabin. I'll tell you."

BarbaRossa and I went to his cabin, and I was surprised to see Guru waiting for us. He was sitting in the captain's chair!

"What's he doing here?" I asked. "Isn't he supposed to be in the dungeon with the Yagas?"

"Guru knows the dangers of the Zanzibar waters better than anyone," BarbaRossa answered. "In such complicated situations, I trust him more than anybody else. He has developed a plan for recovery of the treasure."

"Levend," Guru said in his soft, calm voice, "you taught me something very important during our time in the dungeon. You said friendship isn't about asking someone to be your friend, but about living through experiences together. Well, this is one of those times that will test and grow our friendship. Please trust me and follow the plan I have prepared for you. I want you to come out safely, and I'm not the only one."

I assumed he meant Giant Yang Yang and Little Fan Fan,

and the reminder of their friendship made me feel hopeful. Though BarbaRossa glared at him, Guru had earned my trust. I felt that he would do everything he could to protect me.

"This is a very dangerous mission," he continued. "This isn't Yalova; the Zanzibar Treasure is sitting at the bottom of the sea, a thousand feet below us. You'll need to go deeper very slowly to make sure water pressure doesn't crush your seabubble. If you sense it's starting to fail, return to the surface. We lost nine pirates to sharks and lobster-popsters the last time we tried to recover the treasure. Of course, you don't need to worry about the sharks. BarbaRossa told me about your little adventure earlier. However, lobster-popsters have an incredible grip, and I'd be surprised if anything could protect you for long. As soon as you see one, you need to come up immediately."

"What am I supposed to do if one chases me?" I asked. This wasn't going to be an easy task.

"There's only one thing you *can* do: swim faster," Guru replied. "Get out of there as soon as possible. Listen to me, I don't want you to be there any longer than you need to be. When you get to the bottom of the sea, look around. There should be twelve treasure chests near the shipwreck. You'll notice right away that each of the chests has either gold or silver letters on them. Focus on the chests with gold letters. The chests are too heavy for you to bring to the surface, so you will carry a rope with you. When you find the chests, tie this rope around them, and we'll pull them up."

"I understand, Guru," I replied. "I'll only go after the chests with gold letters."

"There should be six chests with golden letters," reiterated BarbaRossa. "After you find those, you can start collecting the others."

We left the cabin, and I pulled my seabubble on. From the mumbling and shifting on deck, I learned a surprising fact about the pirates. Just like BarbaRossa, most of them didn't know how to swim! While all the pirates were looking at me in awe, I jumped in the water.

I dove deeper and deeper, and as soon as I reached the seabed, I saw something shining. I swam closer and saw that it was one of the chests, already cracked open. I could even see the shiny objects within, but when I looked at the lid of the chest, there was the silver letter "J". I didn't understand why BarbaRossa didn't prize the chest, but his instructions had been clear, and I didn't want to risk my life for some stupid treasure. I moved on.

I swam around a little, finding another chest. It wasn't open, but it had the gold letter "I" on its lid. I tied the rope, tugged it twice, and they pulled the chest up.

Soon after, I found a second chest with a gold letter "E" on it. The next had the letter "C."

I started to wonder what the letters might mean. *IEC*?

I got to the next one, which boasted an "E."

The next one had a "B," and the last one had an "N" on it. "IECEBN?"

Unable to think straight at that depth, the puzzle was too complicated for me. I knew, though, that at least the first part of my mission was complete. Now, I could start work on the other chests. I swam toward the "J" chest and saw something moving behind its lid.

It was shaped like a lobster but the size of a small boat. Until it moved, I'd thought it was part of the ship, mistaking the beautiful patterns on its shell for carvings in the wood. As it scuttled towards me, claws spread wide, I saw that it had built a nest right behind the chest.

I started to swim away immediately, but the lobster-popster was fast. Its arm shot out, and it grabbed one of my legs in a vice-like claw. It felt like being tickled, but I knew that if I could feel it through the seabubble, the monster was about to pinch a hole. I kicked out, aiming for the soft underbelly, but the lobster-popster held firm.

The tickling sensation intensified, and I whispered my good-byes to Ayshin and Auntie Aysun. Just as I thought it was over, the tickling lessened. I looked up to see that the lobster-popster's eyes had swiveled away, locked on three sharks that circled in the distance. For a second, I wondered why the huge lobster-popster was scared of sharks, but then it looked back to the nest and I understood: it was worried about its eggs! I kicked out again, and the lobster-popster looked around just as I managed to grab the rope dangling from the ship. It yanked on my leg, once, twice… and the men on the ship started pulling me up. They certainly weren't stronger than the lobster-popster, but with the sharks getting closer and my seabubble resisting its grip, it was enough to persuade the monster that I wasn't worth its trouble. It let go and, as fast as I could, I swam for the surface. Thankfully, the pirates were waiting, and they pulled me up onto the deck.

I climbed out of my seabubble and found that the pirates had already put the chests side by side. This time, they were in the right order: "BENICE." The treasure chests spelled the name of BarbaRossa's wife. Zhan Yaga and Jamie Yaga were dancing around the treasure chests, happy as usual and entertaining the pirates. Before I'd even dried myself, Zamora stamped over to me.

"Where the hell is the rest of the treasure? Where are the other chests? Why didn't you bring up all the chests?"

I looked around, but BarbaRossa wasn't on the deck. I realized that was probably why Zamora was trying to get as much information from me as possible. I looked Zamora in the eye.

"I was attacked by a lobster-popster, okay? That's the whole story."

Before I could say anything else, BarbaRossa came out of the captain's quarters. Guru was standing next to him.

"Calm down, Zamora," the captain said. "You need to trust the boy a little bit. He has no reason to lie; he's been a good, obedient dog for us, so far."

I couldn't believe he'd called me a dog. If that was a pirate's sense of humor, I didn't like it.

"Okay, witches," BarbaRossa called to the Yagas, "what are you waiting for? Open the treasure chests. Bring me some good luck."

The Yagas performed a few more dancing circles, twerked their butts, and opened the first chest. It was empty. It was odd to see such mystical beings look so baffled; they certainly hadn't brought BarbaRossa any luck. One after another, all the treasure chests came up empty, containing nothing more than seawater and barnacles. Pirates started to holler at each other. Where was the Zanzibar Treasure? They knew for sure that the chests had been full when Jamoka's ship sank.

"We shouldn't have let the Yagas open the chests," shouted one pirate. "They made the treasure disappear!"

"Stop blaming my wife, Half-Baked! This is clearly one of BarbaRossa's tricks," yelled Zamora. "You're hiding something from us, BarbaRossa. You promised to recover the Zanzibar Treasure, you brought us all the way here, but all you have to show for it is empty treasure chests. How can you explain this?"

Apart from Half-Baked, who was still smarting from being yelled at, the men had begun to growl their support one way or the other, and I sensed that something bad was going to happen. Those already loyal to Zamora were growing restless and grabbing their swords. There were fewer of them than the regular crew, but they certainly looked like the stronger side. Abdi began to gather BarbaRossa's men, ordering them to prepare their weapons.

It was an argument that made no sense, because BarbaRossa was as confused as the others. He moved to the chests, inspecting them one by one. He ran his fingers around the lids and bottoms, checking to make sure the treasure couldn't have fallen out. He spent extra time on the "C" chest, completely ignoring Zamora and his men. After he finished his inspection, he looked like he was satisfied. He stood up and whispered a few words to Guru. Then, he walked toward Zamora's men.

"What's the problem here, mates? When I came here, I promised you I'd recover the Zanzibar Treasure. This is only half of the loot. There are still six more treasure chests at the bottom of the sea, waiting for us. The boy said he was chased by a lobster-popster and couldn't get all of them out, but when the time is right, we'll send him again and get the remaining treasure."

"But Captain BarbaRossa," said Half-Baked, "how did the Yagas make the treasure disappear?"

"You have to answer Half-Baked, BarbaRossa," yelled another pirate. "How did the treasure disappear?"

"Don't blame me, mates," cried BarbaRossa. "Zamora must have taken it before he sank the *Falcon's Heart.*"

Zamora's men gasped. The captain had just implied that Zamora had killed his own father. Was it possible?

"You lie, BarbaRossa," thundered Zamora. "You accuse me of killing my father just to cover your own theft. *You* are the one who stole the treasure. Give it back!"

As he talked, I was confused to see that Zamora was staring at me. With a start, I realized why; he believed I had partnered with BarbaRossa, perhaps even hiding the treasure at the bottom of the sea before bringing empty chests to the surface.

"Don't look at me!" I protested. "I don't want to be in the middle of this mess. I'm not working with anybody aboard this ship. No offense, but I don't like you, Zamora, and I definitely hate BarbaRossa. He kidnapped me and brought me here by force! All I want to do is go home. I'm sick of all of you. I dove to the bottom of the sea and found the chests. I didn't have any idea what was, or wasn't, inside them. Think about it! They were hard to open up here; they'd be even harder to open on the seabed. Even if they weren't, I didn't have time to open and empty them all! Look, I held up my end of the bargain. It's time to hold to your pirate oath and send me back to Yalova."

It appeared that Zamora's men were satisfied with my response, but they didn't seem interested in taking me back to Yalova.

"We want payback," cried one of Zamora's men. "You have to deliver us the treasure, BarbaRossa! When an honorable captain makes a promise, he should deliver!"

Their attention had shifted away from me, and I snuck off the deck and tucked myself safely into a corner. I watched the pirates, hoping they'd fight. The idea that they had honor was a joke.

"You and your little boy deserve to be punished," Zamora cried, and before he'd even finished his sentence, his men started to chant.

"Zamora, Zamora, Zamora! *Captain* Zamora!"

Zamora got up on a high point of the deck and looked towards BarbaRossa's men.

"I will give you one more chance to pledge your allegiance to me. Come to my side! I won't spare anyone who fights for this half-man."

Nobody moved.

"Abdi?" Zamora said, gesturing him to come to his side.

Abdi locked eyes with BarbaRossa. To BarbaRossa's disbelief, he defiantly walked to Zamora's side.

"Abdi?" BarbaRossa said, looking stunned. His best friend from childhood, best man at his wedding, and his confidant during all these years was betraying him. "Why?"

"You don't have to know the answer BarbaRossa," Abdi said, shrugging. "You'll be dead soon."

Before too long, I heard war screams, and the groups collided. All I could hear was yelling and the clashing of swords. It was a vicious fight, and pirates from both sides fell. I thought I was safe, but one of Zamora's men began stumbling over to my hiding place. There was no way I could protect myself, so I was relieved to hear a friendly voice calling my name.

"Levend! Levend, come here!"

It was Giant Yang Yang. He was standing next to some empty gunpowder barrels. I lowered myself and crawled toward him.

"That guy was coming to kill me!" I told Giant Yang Yang.

"I doubt it; they really will honor the pirate's oath. In a brawl like this, though, accidents can happen. Get inside," he said, pointing to a fifty-five-gallon barrel. "This is a good place to hide during a fight. Don't come out until the battle is over! You wouldn't survive more than two minutes out there."

"Hey, where's Little Fan Fan?" I asked, sliding into the barrel. Giant Yang Yang looked at me and twirled his mustache.

"Where do you think, landlubber? He's on the deck, fighting. A real pirate would never miss an opportunity to fight!"

It was a good thing I wasn't a pirate, since I was perfectly happy to stay inside the barrel. Giant Yang Yang drew his sword, and I looked at him in confusion.

"Hey, where are you going?" I asked.

"I'm going to fight for Captain BarbaRossa! You'll be safe inside that barrel. We'll get you out when the time is right."

He ran off, waving his sword, and I ducked inside the barrel, watching the rest of the fight through a small hole.

Swords clashed and punches landed, but after a while, the fighting stopped. I waited hours for Little Fan Fan and Giant Yang Yang to come, but nobody did. The ship was silent and, as darkness fell, I got the feeling that the *Falcon's Blood* was drifting aimlessly on the currents. The only sound I could hear was the splash of waves. I was on a ghost ship. My friends Little Fan Fan and Giant Yang Yang must have died in the fight! I slipped out of the barrel and walked carefully around the deck to see the carnage. My worst fear was confirmed; there wasn't a living soul to be seen. My friendship with Little Fan Fan, Giant Yang Yang, and Guru had been just about to blossom, but I'd lost them in a stupid pirate battle. I felt hopeless and started to cry, but I knew I couldn't just do nothing. I had to search every inch of this ship; if my friends were injured, they'd need my help.

I searched and searched, but there was no sign of them. Eventually, I found BarbaRossa. He was badly injured and breathing heavily.

He took a deep breath and whispered, "I love you, my little boy."

I couldn't believe it. He was lying to me, even as he was dying! Ever since we'd landed on the ship, he'd been determined to torture me. He continued to speak softly, and I could barely hear him.

"I'm so sorry for how I treated you, Levend, but it was all necessary. If Zamora had known how much I cared about you, he'd have used you as leverage. I was terrified you wouldn't realize none of us could use the seabubble, but after I was able to swear the pirate oath, things were simpler. I trusted Little Fan Fan and Giant Yang Yang would care for you, and I hoped the Yagas would comfort you at night. Guru, too, played his part." He paused a second to catch his breath. "Levend, I love you. Before I die, I want to give you the greatest treasure a father can give to his son."

I struggled for a moment, wrestling with my confused feelings. But, even as I struggled, I realized that I loved him too. I'd never forgotten how he'd tried to sacrifice himself for me. I wanted to give him one more chance.

"But BarbaRossa, why did you even bring me here in the first place? Why did you put my life in danger? Just for treasure? Was it really worth dying for?"

"I understand you're upset, but I don't have an answer for you. Not today. Perhaps you'll understand when you grow up and fall in love for the first time. The Zanzibar Treasure was definitely worth dying for. I'm sorry I can't explain, but please, before I die, I want to give *you* some treasure. Not all treasures are made of gold and silver, Levend. There are many more priceless treasures you can cherish in your life."

Before he said another word, he passed out. I checked to see that he was still breathing, wondering what kind of treasure he could possibly give me. There was nothing valuable in the chests on the deck, and I was the only one who could get the treasure at the bottom of the sea. For now, I had bigger things to worry about, like finding my friends. I dragged BarbaRossa to a shaded area and gave him some water, then I started to look for survivors. I could only hope that, by some miracle, Little Fan Fan and Giant Yang Yang might be alive.

ZHAN AND JAMIE YAGA

CHAPTER ELEVEN

SURPRISE VISITORS

Once I realized that BarbaRossa and I were the only survivors, I started worrying. How was I going to survive aboard a pirate ship in the middle of the ocean? An injured BarbaRossa wouldn't be much help. This was a bad situation.

The weather, at least, was clear. There was no wind, and I didn't worry about steering the ship, letting it just drift with the currents. After a short time worrying about my options, I heard noise coming from the captain's cabin. I ran toward the noise, but before opening the door, I put my ear against it and tried to listen. There was definitely somebody inside. I slowly opened the door, ready to defend myself.

"Benice, I love you," said Toy.

"Oh, Toy, it's you," I said. It wasn't what I'd been hoping for, but at least it was company. "Glad to see you alive."

"Aren't you glad to see me, as well?" came another voice.

"Who's there?" I asked, surprised.

"Who else do you expect to survive this carnage? Smartest guy on the ship, maybe?"

"Guru? Is that you?"

"Of course!"

I grinned, laughing in relief.

"Well, yeah, I *am* glad to see you too, Guru. Any idea how we're going to survive out here?"

"Relax. Did you really think Zamora was running this ship? He knew nothing! I'm the brain of this ship; I know how to steer and navigate. Without me, Zamora would have crashed the *Falcon's Blood* into a lighthouse long ago."

Smiling, I went downstairs to check the food supply. Fortunately, pirates could be trusted to take care of themselves, and there was plenty of food. One less problem to worry about!

Satisfied, I went back upstairs to the captain's deck. Guru was already at the helm of the *Falcon's Blood*, but now I wondered how two teenagers could steer a huge pirate ship. Guru seemed more than competent, but what would happen if there was a storm? Suddenly, I felt hopeless again; our only chance was to find another ship or an island.

I stared at the horizon, wishing for help, and almost immediately saw a black dot! Could this be our savior? I ran to find BarbaRossa's binoculars. The black dot looked like a ship, but it was still too far away to identify. I was so tired; I thought it might be a mirage. Overcome, I slumped to the floor and passed out.

When I woke up, the sun was shining brightly. I squinted and struggled to stand up. Looking to my right, I couldn't believe my eyes. There was another ship right next to us! At first, I was overjoyed to see that somebody had come to save us, but my happiness didn't last. I looked up at the flag waving on the mast of the ship; it was exactly the same as that of the *Falcon's Blood*. Great. I'd survived one gang of pirates, only to be killed by another! Worse, once they found out about the Zanzibar Treasure, I'd have to go seabubbling for treasure again. My luck was running dry.

It didn't take too long for one of the pirates from the other ship to swing across to the *Falcon's Blood*.

"Where is BarbaRossa?" he shouted, running over to me.

"He's injured," I said, pointing and running over to the captain, "but he's alive."

The pirate was an Orhun and only a little older than me, so I was surprised he knew BarbaRossa.

The pirate carefully checked BarbaRossa's injuries and asked, "Are either of you responsible for this?"

"No," Guru and I replied simultaneously.

"We have nothing to do with this fight," I continued. "Zamora and his pirates did it while I was hiding inside a barrel!"

"Both of you, lie down on the deck, do not move," he instructed. "What are your names?"

"My name is Guru. He is Levend."

The pirate was careful in his moves. He wanted to differenti-ate friend from foe.

"Did anybody else survive this carnage?"

"Just the two of us and BarbaRossa," I said, but before he could reply, we were interrupted by someone yelling from the ship.

"Hey! Is everything okay over there?" called a familiar voice.

"No, there was a huge battle!" the pirate shouted back. "Only three men survived."

"Is Levend okay?"

"Yes, he's okay."

Hoppalaa! I was stunned. How did they know my name?

"How's BarbaRossa?"

"He's alive, but just barely," replied the pirate. "There's also a young Nevar named Guru. There are no other survivors."

"What about my twins?" screamed another voice, a woman's voice. "Can you see them?"

"I can't, Mrs. Lu."

As soon as he'd finished his sentence, we heard the sound of falling barrels. The pirate grabbed his sword.

"Who's there? Show yourself!"

Two white flags came up, waved by Little Fan Fan and Giant Yang Yang.

"Hey, Little Fan Fan and Giant Yang Yang," said the pirate,

"I was worried about you! I'm glad to see you guys alive. Hey, Little Fan Fan, you grew up very fast, you're as big as Giant Yang Yang now! Of course, I had no doubt you'd both have excellent mustaches."

This pirate seemed to know everybody on the ship! How did he know Little Fan Fan and Giant Yang Yang?

"Who are you?" I asked him.

"I'm sorry," he said. "I didn't properly introduce myself. My name is Orion."

"I'm not interested in your name," I said angrily. "How do you know the people on this ship?"

He didn't answer, but gave me a warm, friendly smile. I took BarbaRossa's binoculars and focused on the other ship. How was this possible? What was going on?

"Hoppalaa! How did *you* get here?" I cried out.

So far, the kids of Yalova have listened to me attentively, but now they're distracted by two duetting parrots. While one of them screeches, "Benice, I love you! Benice, I love you!" the other sings, "You are the most beautiful woman in the world, Benice!"

"That's got to be Toy!" one of the kids yells, covering his ears. "Mr. Levend, you didn't tell us how bad Toy's singing is. Please, make her stop!"

I hush the kids.

"For Mrs. Benice, that was the most beautiful sound." I turn and, exactly as I expected, discover that the parrots are perched on the shoulders of two strange-looking women. "Okay, Jamie Yaga and Zhan Yaga, how long have you been listening to the story?"

"Pretty much from the beginning. You've done a wonderful job talking about yourself and your friends, selfish boy, but you didn't tell much of Benice and BarbaRossa's love story."

The Yalova kids are clearly amazed to see the Yaga ladies.

"Mr. Levend, are these ladies really the same Yagas from the dungeon?"

"Yes, they are."

"But weren't they killed in the fight?"

"Ah, no, they were sensible enough to hide. Not that we knew at the—"

Jamie coughs and furrows her brow. I turn back to the Yagas.

"Apologies, ladies. Let me introduce you to my new friends from Yalova. These kids are some of the best fishermen in the world."

The kids are already trying to convince the Yagas to show their dance moves. Though the Yagas playfully reject their requests, the kids start to hum a Yalova folk song. Sure enough, the Yagas start to shake their bodies.

The dance goes on for a while, and we all join in. I may be a grown man, but I'm no more immune to the Yagas than when I was a boy. As it finishes, the kids take their spots around me.

"Mr. Levend, who is the talented parrot? How come you didn't mention it in your story?"

Before I can answer, Zhan Yaga interrupts, "The name of that parrot is Beacon. And I already told you kids, Levend is missing most of BarbaRossa's story."

"Not true," I object.

"You sure did, Levend," Jamie agrees. "I think it's better for Orion to tell the rest of the story anyway. He knows more about Benice and BarbaRossa than you."

Actually, that sounds fine to me. After all, he needs to make up with the kids.

"Orion," I ask, "do you mind telling the rest of the story?"

"I'd be happy to. Kids, do you remember where Mr. Levend left off?"

"You boarded Mr. Levend's ship to save him from the pirates, and that was the first time you met him," comes the reply.

"Don't forget to tell us about Beacon, Mr. Orion!"

"Of course, I will tell you everything. But, I must start my story when Levend left Yalova with Mr. Ben."

YOUNG BENICE AND BARBAROSSA

CHAPTER TWELVE

BACK TO YALOVA

After seeing Levend leave with Mr. Ice, Ayshin, Zhu Zhu, and Zhen Zhen went back home. Ayshin went upstairs and confirmed that her brother's seabubble was missing. She asked Zhu Zhu whether Levend had been carrying a backpack and realized her worst fears had come true. She knew now that she should have done more to stop Levend, but it was too late. Although she'd known Mr. Ice was up to no good, she hadn't said anything. She hoped that maybe, just maybe, Levend would return from the fishing trip in time for dinner.

Levend wasn't back for dinner, and people started to panic. Ayshin told them Levend was probably fishing with Mr. Ice. Just like before, all of Yalova started to worry, but this time, Levend really was missing. The fishermen, including Mr. Ice, always returned to the iskele before dark. But this time it was obvious that either Mr. Ice or Levend, or both of them, were injured or in trouble out on the sea. The prevailing opinion was that Levend had been kidnapped by Mr. Ice, and that he was probably chopped into pieces already. Despite all the good work he had done for the kids, people quickly went back to thinking of him as a pirate.

Everybody was mad at Ayshin. Why hadn't she asked for help? The villagers could have started looking for Levend earlier! It was too dark now, and a rescue party would have to wait until sunrise.

I arrived in Yalova on the day Levend disappeared with Mr. Ice. My ship quietly entered the harbor and anchored at a distance from the beach. I came ashore in a row boat, accompanied by three of my men. We approached two young Nevar girls sitting under the trees by the beach.

"Hi girls, how are you doing?"

The girls didn't answer. After all, we were strangers to them.

"Don't be alarmed," I said. "I'm not going to hurt you. I just wanted to find a friend of mine. Can you help me?"

The girls still didn't answer. They looked like they were thinking about running away.

"My friend's name is Levend. Do you know where he lives?" As soon as the girls heard Levend's name, they started to pay attention. "My name is Orion. What are your names?"

The girls remained silent, but I could tell I had gained their attention, and what was more, that they knew Levend.

"I really need to see Levend. He may be in danger. I'm here to help."

The girls already knew Levend was in trouble, and this seemed like a real chance to help.

"My name is Zhu Zhu," said one of them. "This is my sister, Zhen Zhen. We don't know Levend very well, but his sister Ayshin is a good friend. We can take you to her house."

"Yes, thank you. Please, hurry!"

We ran together, and soon we were knocking on Ayshin's door. Ayshin came rushing downstairs to open it, only to discover a sailor standing at the threshold. My men were on the lookout at the curbside, but Ayshin couldn't see Zhu Zhu or Zhen Zhen.

"Who are you, knocking on my door in the middle of the night?" Ayshin asked suspiciously.

"My name is Orion Rossa," I said with a soft, polite voice. "I am BarbaRossa's son."

Orion draws a breath to continue, but the Yalova kids can't hold it in.

"You're Mr. Ben's son! Why didn't you tell us? We thought he was dead!"

"I am alive and well, kids. Let me continue."

Ayshin wasn't so happy to meet me.

"You're the son of the most vicious pirate the world has ever seen! How dare you knock on my door? Go back to where you came from."

She slammed the door in my face, but I knocked again.

"Can you open the door, please? I'm sure I'm at the right place."

"Go away! I don't have anything to do with pirates."

"Ayshin, open the door!" cried Zhu Zhu.

"He knows Levend," added Zhen Zhen. "He may be able to help us find him."

As soon as she heard Levend's name, Ayshin quickly opened the door.

"How do you know my GeGe's name? Do you know where he is?"

"I was hoping to find him right here in Yalova. Is he missing?"

"Yes, my brother is missing. He went fishing with Mr. Ice and never came back."

"Mr. Ice?" I asked. "Does this Mr. Ice have only one eye, one hand, and one leg?"

"Yes."

"Well, I have some news for you. That fisherman's name is not Mr. Ice. Your brother is with my father, BarbaRossa."

"I knew it," Ayshin said. "I should never have trusted that man. Do you realize your father kidnapped an innocent child? Everybody in this town will go after that fugitive tomorrow!"

"The villagers will be wasting their time," I replied immediately. "There is no way they'll be able to track down BarbaRossa on the high seas. He was the best sailor ever. He's probably already out of the Sea of Marmara and has reached the ocean."

"You didn't bring much good news to us, Mr. Orion," said Auntie Aysun, who was standing behind Ayshin.

"This may sound strange," I replied, "but even though BarbaRossa was the most vicious pirate that ever lived, he was probably the best father that ever lived, as well."

"He kidnapped my GeGe!" snapped Ayshin. "He is a pirate! He destroyed many lives! How can you say he's the best father?"

"I can explain. May I come in? I *can* help you find Levend, but I also need your help to find my father. We need each other."

Ayshin looked at Auntie Aysun for permission. She nodded.

"Okay," said Ayshin. "You can come in."

"I need to talk to these folks," I yelled to my men. "I'll be okay. You wait outside until I return."

I went inside with Zhu Zhu and Zhen Zhen and settled near the fireplace. Auntie Aysun was always nice to visitors, even the sons of pirates. She went to the kitchen and brought some hot tea.

"Okay, Mr. Orion," she said, "tell us what you know. How can we save Levend?"

THIEF ZAMORA

CHAPTER THIRTEEN

BENICE AND BARBAROSSA'S STORY

was excited to be one step closer to finding my father, but now I needed to solve the mystery of Levend. Why had my father taken him? What was so special about this kid? I believed that my father would never kidnap a child, and so I also knew there must be a very good reason for the current situation. I took a sip of hot tea and started to tell my parents' story. I had to earn the trust of Ayshin and Auntie Aysun; I had to convince them that my father had taken Levend for a good reason, and that he wouldn't hurt him. If I couldn't earn their trust, I would never find my father.

"BarbaRossa had a very unfortunate life," I began. "You

probably already know that he lost his one eye, one hand, and one leg when he was very young. He had a rough childhood without parents or relatives to take care of him, and people treated him badly. They mocked him, saying that with one eye, one hand, and one leg, he had the natural talent to be a beggar. But he had dignity, he worked hard, and he overcame many difficulties. Even though he slept on the streets, he still attended school. He made a little money to survive, but he never begged. He worked whenever he could."

"A sad childhood does not justify kidnapping my nephew," interrupted Auntie Aysun.

"I don't mean to make BarbaRossa's upbringing an excuse," I said, "but rather to show that BarbaRossa *is* a good man, so you don't need to be as worried as you are. Take his name, for instance! I wasn't surprised to hear he had called himself Ben Ice. That is my mother's name, split in half. She was named 'Benice', you see. He probably called himself Ben Ice to hear people say her name."

I paused for a moment, ready for Auntie Aysun's interruption, but she was clearly touched by BarbaRossa's cleverness and passion.

"My mother, Benice," I continued, "was the most beautiful girl in my hometown, Gemlyk. Everybody wanted to marry her. So many rich people: businessmen, artists, noblemen, even princes knocked on her door! I asked her how she chose

BarbaRossa out of all her suitors. Her answer was just three words: 'I loved him'. She wasn't looking for money or fame; she wanted to marry the person with the best heart, someone who would truly love her on the good days *and* the bad days. Since I had not met my father, she wanted to tell me everything about him. She told me stories about him every night before I went to bed."

"Orion, excuse me for interrupting," said Ayshin, "but how can you tell me that he's the best father in the world if you haven't even met him! What kind of father was he to have deserted you and your mom? He sounds more like a coward!"

"Please excuse her, Orion. She is worried about her brother," added Auntie Aysun, "but she is right. You have some explaining to do."

"I understand your concerns," I replied, "but let me explain. Now, where was I?"

"You were talking about your mom," Ayshin replied.

"Oh, yes! She especially enjoyed talking about the day she met BarbaRossa..."

On that day, she came out of an expensive restaurant with Prince Maganda. BarbaRossa and his best friend Abdi were working at the restaurant entrance. While Abdi was cleaning the windows on a ladder, BarbaRossa was wiping the floors with his good hand, and my mother noticed him. She went over and asked, "What are you doing here?"

"I am working here, ma'am," BarbaRossa responded.

The prince didn't want to waste his time with common people. After all, he was a nobleman! He opened his wallet, took some money, and threw it at BarbaRossa.

"Apparently, you're not much good at what you do," he said. "You've been trying to clean this spot for the last thirty minutes and still haven't finished. Why don't you stop, go sit on a street corner, open a handkerchief, and do something you're good at? You're despicable, crawling on the floor like this."

Abdi came down from his ladder and took a few steps toward Maganda to teach him a lesson, but Maganda's goons easily stopped him before he got any closer.

BarbaRossa didn't even have a wooden leg at that time. He struggled to stand up and look the prince in the eye. My mother liked to say that when those two men stared at each other, the prince had all the money he could want, but no heart, and BarbaRossa didn't have any money, but he had dignity.

BarbaRossa told Prince Maganda, "Sir, I don't want your money. I never accepted money from anybody. I work for a living; I work very hard, and I do the best I can. It is true I am not as fast as others, but I do my job well, and I finish what I start. I make little money, but little is enough for me. I never, ever felt the need to sell my dignity."

After their first encounter, my mother's heart belonged to BarbaRossa. She told me that she fell in love with my dad the moment he stood up and looked the prince in the eye. He didn't even need to say a single word. She didn't care about his missing eye, hand, or leg. He was the one for her.

She encouraged him to get a wooden leg and learn how to use his hook to become a blacksmith, and he partnered with Abdi to open a little shop. BarbaRossa became the best blacksmith in town, making iron tools, furniture, and kitchen utensils. They got married a couple of years later, and their love grew as they faced the struggles of life together. They couldn't have a baby for a long time. My dad gave two parrots to Benice as a present, meant to entertain her while he was at work. One of the parrots was Beacon, and the other was Toy. Beacon was so talented; she could fly to faraway places and memorize many words. Benice trained Beacon to take messages and lunch to BarbaRossa while he was working at his shop. Unfortunately, Toy wasn't as talented. It took BarbaRossa a long time, but he finally taught Toy to say just four words: "Benice, I love you."

Many years later, my mother finally got pregnant and they started to prepare for a baby. They were the happiest couple in the world!

"That baby was you, right?" asked Zhen Zhen. She was enthralled by the story, and eager to help me. Of course, I would still have to win over Ayshin and Auntie Aysun.

"That's correct, Zhen Zhen. The baby they were expecting was me. Unfortunately, my parents' happiness didn't last long. Before she gave birth, my mom got sick. Doctors told BarbaRossa that her only chance for survival was Zanzibar Elixir…"

BarbaRossa couldn't accept the death of the love of his life and his unborn child. He stepped outside, not knowing how to save his wife. He didn't even know where Zanzibar was. A few minutes later, he saw a muscular Jynx man running toward him. He was carrying one big and one small package, one under each arm. He told BarbaRossa that he was running away from a thief who had tried to steal his bags. He begged BarbaRossa to help him. He looked to the top of the hill and, indeed, he saw someone was chasing the man. He told the man to hide behind some bushes.

A few seconds later, an angry man came running down the hill. He stopped right next to BarbaRossa, breathing heavily.

"有没有看到刚才有个人提着两个袋子跑过去了?" he asked.

"Calm down, please. I can't understand you. Who are you? What do you want?"

"我是吴昊, 这个疯子偷走了我的双胞胎儿子·凡凡和飏飏," the man continued.

"Fan Fan? Yang Yang?" BarbaRossa asked. "What are you talking about? Speak slowly and say something I can understand."

The man realized he wasn't being understood and did his best to reply in kind.

"'I am a thief. Steal babies. I will kill him. Two bags."

The guy looked worried, but he also admitted he was a thief and ready to kill somebody. This lined up with the first man's story, and BarbaRossa decided to send the angry man in the wrong direction.

"Yes, I saw a man carrying something in his hands. He ran that way." He gestured and sent the angry man the wrong way.

After the angry man disappeared, the man with the packages came out of the bushes.

"Thank you for saving my life," he said.

"No problem."

"What are you doing out here, all by yourself?"

"I need to find a way to Zanzibar, but I don't even know where it is!"

"It's your lucky day, mister. Do you see those two ships, there?"

"What about them?"

"Those ships are going to Zanzibar, and I'm already a passenger! I know the captain well, and I'm sure he would be willing to return the favor you have done me and take you to Zanzibar with us."

BarbaRossa couldn't believe his luck. He immediately accepted the offer. He told Benice to hang on and protect their baby, and promised that he would go to Zanzibar, find the elixir, and bring it back to her. They knew it might take a long time for his return, and that it would be unbearable to spend that much time away from each other, but what choice did he have?

BarbaRossa told her to look at the brightest constellation in the sky every night. He would do the same, wherever he was in the world. That constellation was Orion, and it's visible from any point on earth. Benice promised him that she would look for Orion every night, and in that promise, they found my name. They would be bound together by Orion, night and day.

BarbaRossa and his new friend arrived at the beach. A rowboat was waiting for them, and they got in and started to row toward the ships.

At the most unexpected time, a bird landed on BarbaRossa's shoulder and screamed, "Benice, I love you!"

He didn't even look up.

"I knew that you wouldn't leave me alone in this journey, Toy, but you were supposed to stay behind and tell my wife the only magic words you know."

Nevertheless, he was happy that he would have a companion during his quest.

BARBAROSSA AND ZAMORA

CHAPTER FOURTEEN

WELCOME TO FALCON'S HEART

As BarbaRossa rowed away from the beach, a large crowd began to gather. They were yelling "thieves" and "pirates". Some even jumped in their boats and chased BarbaRossa and the stranger. Although BarbaRossa suspected he was helping the wrong person, he didn't have any choice but to row as fast as he could. The two ships were going to Zanzibar, and he had to be on one of them. Any delay might mean his wife's death.

They arrived at the ships ahead of the villagers, and both vessels had already pulled up their anchors. As promised, the ships waited for them, and each had let down a Jacob's ladder for BarbaRossa and his friend.

"There are two ships, here. One of them is called the *Falcon's*

Heart, the other is called the *Falcon's Blood*. Which one should we board?"

"The *Falcon's Heart*!" replied the man. "Captain Jamoka is on that ship."

Each man gathered a package and carefully climbed aboard the *Falcon's Heart*. When BarbaRossa looked back, he saw dozens of villager boats chasing them. As the boats drew closer, villagers started to fire guns at them! He didn't know the nature of his crime, but he knew it was likely he would be a fugitive for the rest of his life. There was no going back to his hometown now.

"BarbaRossa, we saw you getting onto that ship with that Jynx," they yelled. "You better not show your face in Gemlyk ever again!"

Thankfully, the ship's crew didn't have any intention of fighting. They just wanted to leave town as soon as possible. Jamoka started to give instructions to the crew.

"Ahoy, mates! Anchors away! There's no treasure and no revenge to be had, so we'll leave them with their lives!"

BarbaRossa looked up at the ship's mast. He saw the Jolly Roger and, at that moment, he realized he was on a pirate ship. The pirates were far faster than the boats chasing them, and they sailed away from them with ease.

After reaching safety, Captain Jamoka yelled, "Where are the idiots who got us in trouble with the villagers?"

BarbaRossa and his friend stood up. They moved toward the middle of the deck, and the rest of the pirates made a circle around them. There was no question that Jamoka was going to punish them; he just didn't know what form that punishment would take.

"Zamora, my absent-minded son," Jamoka bellowed, approaching the pair. "I'm not surprised it's you again. How many times are you going to get into trouble? I hope you at least brought me something valuable from the village. Open the packages!"

Everybody, including BarbaRossa, was expecting gold, jewelry, or money.

"You're going to like what you see, Father," said Zamora. He opened them both. Inside one was a small baby, inside the other, a big baby.

"Why did you bring the small baby? Haven't I told you only to steal big, healthy babies?"

"The little one was next to the big one. He was kind of cute, and they seemed inseparable. I just grabbed them both!"

BarbaRossa realized then that the man chasing Zamora had been the father looking for the man who stole his children.

"You're never going to learn how to pillage, my son," said Jamoka. "You picked up a little baby because he was cute? You're an idiot! And who is this half-man you brought to my ship?"

"I needed somebody to help me escape the angry mob," explained Zamora.

"Of all the men who could help you row a boat, you picked a man with one eye, one hand, and one leg?" laughed Jamoka. "Was that a smart decision, my son?" At this point, everybody on the deck was laughing at Zamora. "Look, *we* are the pirates, okay? We're the bad guys! Those villagers should never have scared you. Now, throw the small baby and the invalid into the sea."

He turned back and started walking toward his cabin. This was not a fair punishment; BarbaRossa and a little baby sentenced to death, while the idiot responsible got away scot-free. BarbaRossa wasn't ready to accept his death sentence, so he made a bold proposal.

"Jamoka, turn back!" he called. He had grown up with insults, so Jamoka's hard words had not upset him. "I know that you are the king of the high seas. All I want is for you to be fair with me. What if I prove to you not once but twice that I am worthy of staying on this ship? Would you let me and the little baby live?"

Jamoka's response was clear.

"It's a deal, half-man. I can't afford to have useless men on the ship. It's the rule of the high seas: the weak die. I hope you understand."

"I understand, and I respect the rules of a pirate ship. I'll prove to you that I can be helpful." He strode over to one of the pirates. "Give me your sword," he said. The pirate hesitated, but

BarbaRossa repeated, "Give me your sword. You're not scared of me, are you? After all, I'm just a half-man, according to your captain." Jamoka nodded his permission, and BarbaRossa took the sword and lifted it up into the air. "What is this?" Nobody answered. "Anybody? Can anybody tell me what this is?"

"It's a sword!" cried one pirate, and everybody looked at him.

"That was a rhetorical question, you moron, you're not supposed to answer," said another pirate. "No wonder your name is Half-Baked."

"I thought he didn't even know what a sword was!" protested Half-Baked.

"Well, Jamoka," continued BarbaRossa, "your man calls this a sword, but I call it a piece of junk. If I were a pirate, I'd be embarrassed to call this a sword. Not one man here has a decent sword, Jamoka. I think you know that."

Jamoka looked around his crew's swords. BarbaRossa was right; they were in horrible shape. They were bent, chipped, and blunt.

"You've got my attention, half-man," he said. "Now, tell me, what are you going to do about it? They're still good enough to kill you."

Half-Baked chuckled. He was pleased with Jamoka's answer.

"Yeah! Half-Baked with a sword can make a shish kebab from a half-man," he laughed.

"I can make them lighter, stronger, and sharper," said

BarbaRossa, ignoring Half-Baked. "After I fix them, they'll be good enough to turn the tide of a battle. Can one of your men find me a hammer and take me to the kitchen? I'll need only a few minutes."

Jamoka asked Half-Baked to take him to the kitchen, and as they passed by, the pirates made fun of them.

"Hey, easy on the soy sauce!"

"I want my eggs sunny-side-up!"

"Don't forget to wear your pink apron!"

"Don't fully cook Half-Baked!"

BarbaRossa ignored the insults and followed Half-Baked to the kitchen.

BarbaRossa came back a few minutes later, as he had promised. He was holding a gleaming, brand new sword in his hand. He approached one of the pirates and asked him to hand over his bandana. He opened the bandana and threw it up in the air, and then he simply held his sword steady below. The sword was so sharp that, as the bandana fell onto the blade, it split into two pieces and fluttered apart.

"What is this, a magic show?" cried the laughing pirates. "Kill him!"

But Jamoka was impressed. He knew exactly what BarbaRossa had done; a sword that can cut through a falling bandana without any effort is much sharper than a sword that can cut through a thick lug of wood in several hacks.

"Shut up, you morons! You're in the presence of a great black-smith. If I were you, instead of laughing at him, I'd get in line to have my sword sharpened."

"I'm glad you appreciate my skills, Captain," said BarbaRossa. "Indeed, I'm an excellent blacksmith. You're travelling to Zanzibar for treasure, yes? Well, let's say you're successful. Do you have anywhere to put the treasure? I can build treasure chests for you."

"Yes, we are going to Zanzibar for treasure. But, most importantly, I am going to get the Zanzibar Elixir from my old friend Freddie. He has been hiding the elixir from me for too long. I'm going to ferret him out of his hiding place, get the elixir, and be the true ruler of the empire."

BarbaRossa hadn't known more people were chasing the Zanzibar Elixir.

"What are you going to do with this elixir?" he asked.

Jamoka was surprised by the naivety of the question.

"Really? You haven't heard about the elixir? You don't get much news about the world in Gemlyk, do you? That elixir could make me the sole king of the empire."

This revelation meant nothing to BarbaRossa. He didn't care about controlling the empire; he wanted to save his wife.

"What is your name?" Jamoka asked. He was very impressed, and he knew he could use this man.

"My name is BarbaRossa."

"BarbaRossa, you can stay on my ship. You just saved your life. Now, you have to show me *another* skill to save the little baby."

"No, no, no, Captain Jamoka. My smithy skills save the little baby's life, and I have your word on that. *Now*, I will show you the skill that saves my own."

"Show me what else you've got, BarbaRossa; I am a man of my word," said Jamoka.

His face remained still, but he was impressed by the man before him. He was smart, confident, and resolute, all the makings of a good pirate. Nevertheless, he was still a half-man and would be no good in a fight.

"You'll be more than satisfied, Jamoka. I can beat any one of your pirates in a fight. If I win the fight, I will carve out the letter 'B' on the back of your man with my hook. If I lose, you can throw me overboard."

Such an arrogant claim, Jamoka thought. Actually, he had already decided to keep him on the ship. A talented blacksmith would be more than useful. Nevertheless, he wanted to see him fight.

"Who do you want to fight, BarbaRossa? Do you want to fight me, or do you want to pick somebody for yourself?"

"I'm not stupid enough to fight with you, Jamoka. I have to respect the captain. I don't mind fighting any of these losers, though. Now, who wants to be branded with my hook?"

BarbaRossa turned to the pirate crew. They were all look-ing for action. Each of them was licking their chops to teach BarbaRossa a lesson. Who was this mangled city boy, coming to the *Falcon's Heart* and claiming that he could beat anybody on the ship? BarbaRossa made a few circles around the pirates.

"I will pick this man. He looks like your strongest guy." Everybody gasped; BarbaRossa was pointing at Zamora. "I noticed that you called him an idiot for bringing me to this ship but spared him from punishment. Please allow me to lay some punishment on him."

"I have no problem with that," said Jamoka. His son wasn't smart, but he was indeed the strongest pirate on the ship. If he beat the half-man, it would be good entertainment. If he lost to a man with one eye, one hand, and one leg, the embarrass-ment would be a fitting punishment. "Son, do you accept the challenge?"

"Sure," laughed Zamora, grabbing his sword and moving closer to BarbaRossa. "I'll be happy to throw him overboard."

"I was expecting a bare-handed fight, Jamoka," protested BarbaRossa. "I would like to fetch a sword, as well."

"No sword for you," replied Jamoka. "You can use your hook. Besides, he'll need it to put a 'Z' on your back, if he wins the fight."

Actually, BarbaRossa didn't mind the sword. He had devel-oped a trick with his hook to take swords from attackers. Still, he needed his victory to be accepted, and so he put more salt in the wound.

"Okay, moron, you get your sword. I'll fight with my bare hands. Let's go, I'll teach you the lesson of your life!"

"Shut up, half-man," spat Zamora. He was ready to finish the fight with one blow. "Prepare to die."

Zamora charged like an angry bull, swinging his sword in exactly the way BarbaRossa had expected. He ducked the blow easily, then he blocked the sword with his hook, turned in a circle, and twisted it out of Zamora's hand. The crew was shocked by BarbaRossa's agility, and Jamoka grinned at Zamora's frustration. Milking the crowd, BarbaRossa kissed the sword and threw it to Jamoka.

Now it was a bare-handed fight, but that didn't last long, either. BarbaRossa started ripping Zamora's clothes to pieces with his hook. The cloth strips got in Zamora's way, and he grew more and more embarrassed as he was stripped, splitting his attention between fighting, protecting his modesty, and failing to protect himself from BarbaRossa's blows. A few minutes later, Zamora was in his underwear, his face was plastered on the deck, and he was getting the letter "B" carved into his back.

"I was wrong about you, BarbaRossa," said Jamoka. "I apologize. You're going to make a good pirate. In fact, I assign you to the *Falcon's Blood*. At the first opportunity, we'll transfer you both across. Now, salute your captain, who will forever wear your mark."

BarbaRossa felt like cold water had just been dumped over him. Zamora was the captain of the *Falcon's Blood*, and he had just embarrassed him in front of the crew! He looked down at Zamora, knowing he was already planning revenge.

"One more thing. We have a pirate tradition; whoever recruits new pirate babies gets to name them. What do you want to name our youngest pirates?"

"I will call the small one Little Fan Fan and the big one Giant Yang Yang. Is that acceptable?"

"Acceptable, it is."

And so it was.

Ayshin interrupted me, "It's nice that you're sharing your father's sad life story with us, but how is this related to Levend? How can we get Levend back?"

"Levend is in real danger," I said. "He and BarbaRossa are sailing directly into Zamora's hands."

"I *know that!*" cried Ayshin, almost ready to kick me in the groin. "I know he's in danger! You just tell me how we can save my GeGe!"

Zhu Zhu and Zhen Zhen were upset as well. They hugged Ayshin, trying to make her calm down.

"Be quiet, Ayshin," said Auntie Aysun. "Let's listen to what this young man has to say. I believe he's trying to help."

"Thank you, ma'am," I said, and I continued the story.

FREDDIE BULSARA'S STORE

CHAPTER FIFTEEN

ZANZIBAR

The *Falcon's Heart* and the *Falcon's Blood* arrived in Zanzibar. The day before they intended to raid the town, Jamoka sent a small team of pirates ashore in a small rowing boat. He knew that Freddie had disguised himself as a merchant and was running a store named Bulsara's Carpets. As the newest addition to the crew, BarbaRossa was chosen to enter alone and play the customer. He stalked along dark, unfamiliar streets, finally finding the right door and entering to the sound of chimes.

"Welcome to Zanzibar," cried a bombastic voice from behind the counter. "Poor servant of the sailors, Freddie, is at your service."

"And I at yours," BarbaRossa replied, trying to be charming.

Freddie came out from behind the counter toward the lighted area. He was an old Orhun, but a strange-looking one. His upper jaw protruded like an otter's, and there was a big gap between his two front teeth. As soon as he saw BarbaRossa, he realized something was wrong. BarbaRossa wasn't playing his role well.

"The only visitors we see in this town are Jynx pirates and King Korsan's soldiers. You look like a pirate, but you don't talk like one. What brought you here?"

"You're right. I'm neither a pirate nor a soldier; I'm just a visitor looking for a carpet."

"Let me go in the back and bring you out some samples," Freddie replied.

He had no intention of coming back, of course. Disappearing into the back of his shop, he put the precious elixir bottles in his bag and left through the back door. He was a shrewd man and had instantly understood that BarbaRossa didn't have honest intent. Unfortunately, the only thing he didn't know was that Jamoka's pirates were waiting for him. It was a simple trick, but it meant they could be sure that Freddie was carrying all of the elixir. They swiftly took him to the *Falcon's Heart*.

Jamoka was waiting for them on the ship's deck, growing more and more anxious. When he finally met with Freddie, whatever kindness he might have shown was gone.

"It's been a long time, Freddie. I should congratulate you, I suppose, for managing to evade the kings of land and sea. In fact, I suppose I should even thank you for keeping the elixir from Korsan."

"You are both disgraces to this empire," Freddie spat back. "You may have the elixir, but I assure you, you won't be successful. You understand only the smallest part of what that elixir will do to you."

"Shut up, old man," Jamoka replied. "This elixir will give me my youth, and I will be ruler for the next hundred years. I understand *that*." He turned to his pirates. "Take him to the dungeon. BarbaRossa, come with me to the captain's cabin."

BarbaRossa obeyed, surprised to find himself alone in the cabin with Jamoka.

"You didn't disappoint me on your first mission, my talented friend," he said to BarbaRossa. "You can join the other pirates tomorrow to raid the city. Freddie's time has passed, but his warning wasn't bluster. The elixir takes as much as it gives, but it is still desired by our false king. You must keep it a secret, and we'll have to find a way to hide it, for now. I want you to prepare three sets of treasure chests for that purpose. One third of the treasure belongs to the pirates of the *Falcon's Blood*, one third belongs to the pirates of the *Falcon's Heart*, and the remaining third belongs to the captain. We'll fill them with the loot we obtain tomorrow, but I also want you to create secret compartments for the elixir. Can it be done?"

"It can," BarbaRossa replied.

He wasn't interested in raiding the city; in fact, his mind was racing with ways to get the elixir from Jamoka and hurry back to Benice. Once he was out of sight, he ran down to the dungeon, eager to find Freddie and learn about the powers of the elixir.

"Mr. Freddie, I'm so sorry that I did this to you. I know that Jamoka isn't a good person, I'm sure he has bad intentions, but I need you to forgive me for helping him. I had my reasons."

"What reasons?" Freddie sneered.

"Love," replied BarbaRossa.

It was enough to get Freddie's honest attention, and BarbaRossa explained why he wanted the elixir. Freddie listened carefully, touched by Benice and BarbaRossa's story.

"I understand, but if you knew the power of this elixir, you wouldn't hesitate to sacrifice your family for it."

"I'm sorry, but I would do anything to save my wife," BarbaRossa replied.

"You are a determined man, BarbaRossa. It looks like you're determined to steal the elixir from Jamoka, and that can only be a good thing, but you must still keep it safe. If you are to be its guardian, even for your own ends, you must understand the enormous power of the elixir.

"You know that our kings rule the empire for a hundred years, of course, but what you may not know is that it's the elixir that allows them to do so. The Zanzibar Elixir is extracted from a cactus flower that blooms only once every hundred years. The harvested elixir is used to anoint the new king – not only does it ensure good health and youth, but it is a vital part of the ancient crowning ceremony. Korsan may rule the empire, but without the elixir, it won't be for long, and there are many who would never consider him our true ruler without it. I have been able to hide the elixir from both him and Jamoka, saving it for someone worthy of becoming our new ruler."

"So, if I give the elixir to Benice, she'll become our new ruler?" BarbaRossa asked.

"No, not without the proper ceremony," Freddie replied. "If she is as ill as you say, the elixir will do little more than restore her to health. And I suspect she'd be immune to the elixir's side-effects, since so much of its power will be needed to heal her. If you give your wife the elixir, you *will* save her, but you will doom the rest of us.

"For a hundred years, there will be no true king. The empire will remain in chaos, its citizens warring and dying because of your selfish decision. More than that – when used correctly, the elixir's power lives within the ruler for a hundred years before returning to the flower. Some believe that, if the ceremony is not performed, the flower will never bloom again. Do you understand? For the life of one woman, we may never know peace again."

"I understand," said BarbaRossa, "but I... I must save my wife. If I do, at least Jamoka and Korsan cannot rule for long."

"You and I are different breeds BarbaRossa," said Freddie. "I sacrificed my family to prevent Korsan and Jamoka from getting the elixir, you are choosing your family over the entire empire. This may look like a good decision to you now, but history will not treat you kindly."

"I have made my choice. I will take that elixir from Jamoka and give it to my wife," said BarbaRossa.

He left the elixir's former guardian in the dungeon and began, straight away, to build the treasure chests.

DEMISE OF FALCON'S HEART

CHAPTER SIXTEEN

END OF JAMOKA

BarbaRossa watched the pirates return to the *Falcon's Heart* and pile their loot into a mound. Jamoka proudly circled the treasure.

"Bring the treasure chests, master blacksmith."

BarbaRossa brought the eighteen empty chests onto the deck. He had marked six chests with the letters "Z – A – M – O – R – A" cast in bronze, six more with the letters "J – A – M – O – K – A" cast in silver, and another six with the letters "B – E – N – I – C – E" cast in gold. He had followed Jamoka's instructions, adding secret compartments to the final chests and hiding one vial of Zanzibar Elixir in each. He hid the key for these compartments in the chest marked with the letter "C," and he kept the seventh vial for himself.

Jamoka came over to inspect them.

"You did a good job. I'm glad you marked them differently in three groups; it'll be easier to divvy up the treasure. What does 'Benice' mean?"

"That's my wife's name, sir," BarbaRossa answered proudly, and Jamoka nodded in approval.

In a few minutes, he'd gathered the entire crew.

"Listen up, everybody, it's time to divide the treasure. I will choose first and put my one-third share in the chests marked with gold letters. The remainder of the treasure will be divided equally between the crews of the *Falcon's Blood* and the *Falcon's Heart*. Chests marked with the bronze letters will go to the *Falcon's Blood*. Chests marked with the silver letters will remain on the *Falcon's Heart*, along with my own chests."

Every pirate on the ship was happy, except two. BarbaRossa was the first unhappy man. He needed to figure out how to steal the elixir from Jamoka and return to his wife as soon as possible. The second unhappy man was Zamora. He was still reeling from his defeat and his father's humiliating comments. He couldn't accept the embarrassment, and he didn't like that Jamoka had taken all the most valuable treasures. He thought he deserved his own share; after all, he was the captain of the *Falcon's Blood*.

While everybody was drinking, Zamora moved down to the cannon deck. He aimed one of the cannons directly at the soft belly of the *Falcon's Heart*, and then, without any hesitation, he lit the fuse. *Boom!* Everybody was so drunk that none of the pirates on the *Falcon's Blood* even noticed that the cannon had been fired. BarbaRossa ran down to the cannon deck and saw Zamora standing next to the smoking weapon.

"What have you done, you fool?"

"Jamoka messed with my pride and got what he deserved. Do you have a problem with that?"

"No, but you have taken something from me, even without knowing it. I'll tell the crew what you've done and see how *they* feel about it!"

"I'll deny it," spat Zamora, "In fact, I'll say *you* killed my father. They'll believe me over you."

"I don't care, I'll let them decide. I have told the truth ever since I boarded this ship, and they know it as surely as they know you are a jealous fool. They will trust me."

"We'll make a deal," said Zamora, shaken. He wasn't sure, now, who would be believed. "I'll take you back to Gemlyk. I know that you don't want to be a pirate for the rest of your life, and I don't want you on this ship. Deal?"

That made sense to BarbaRossa. He only had one vial of elixir left, and it might just be enough to extend Benice's life for a few months so she could give birth to Orion. He might be unable to save his wife, but he could yet save his child. He accepted Zamora's offer.

The pirates woke the next morning to find the *Falcon's Heart* gone. Zamora lied about what had happened.

"Mates, there was an accident last night aboard the *Falcon's Heart*. Unfortunately, we lost my father and our comrades. They're gone, but they won't be forgotten. Now, we're taking

BarbaRossa back to his hometown. He has to save his wife and child."

In the meantime, back in his hometown, BarbaRossa was a wanted man. As far as the villagers were concerned, he had stolen two babies and become a pirate. They weren't going to forgive him, and they told Benice what her husband had done. They told her to leave, saying she was not welcome in Gemlyk anymore. Benice tried to defend the love of her life and the father of her unborn child, but the villagers wouldn't listen. Her doctor told her that if she went high into the mountains of Altay, she might be able to live longer and give birth to her child, but it would be a dangerous journey. She packed and left town all by herself, telling no one of her plans.

The pirates brought BarbaRossa to the beach on a rowboat. He secretly met Abdi and learned that the villagers wouldn't allow him in town anymore, and that they'd already banished Benice. He was furious. Abdi told him that he tried his best but could not stop the villagers expelling Benice from Gemlyk. BarbaRossa was devastated, and Abdi encouraged him to take his revenge on the villagers. In that instant, he made a decision. He returned to the *Falcon's Blood* with Abdi. He didn't talk to anyone, striding directly to the highest point of the deck.

"From this point onward, I am the captain of this ship," he boomed. "I dare anybody to challenge me."

There was a silence until Half-Baked yelled, "Didn't we just drop you off at your village? Why did you come back?"

He was, and is, a foolish man. Who cared why BarbaRossa had come back? This was a clear mutiny. He wasn't expecting any questions, and he wasn't going to answer to anybody. The pirates either needed to kill him or accept him as the new captain. Everybody looked to Zamora; they didn't care who was captain, except that it must be the strongest man.

Zamora still remembered the beating he had taken. The scar on his back ached, and he knew he would lose another fight. He didn't say anything.

"I am your captain!" BarbaRossa declared again. "Is there anybody here who doesn't accept this? Anybody?"

Nobody dared answer.

"Just what I expected. Mates! Get ready to rule the high seas. A new pirate era will spread across the Marmara Sea and the entire Mediterranean. King Korsan may rule the land, but the high seas belong to me. Pirates fight for either treasure or revenge. Your first fight under my command will be for revenge! I want each and every one of you to go down to this damned village and destroy it. Burn the whole village. I don't want their money, you can have the spoils. They took my precious wife and child away from me. My vengeance will be upon them."

The pirates didn't understand why they had to attack, but they knew to listen to their captain. They razed Gemlyk, and with no clue where Benice could have gone, BarbaRossa started to sail the seas aimlessly. As time passed, he was pulled more and more to the dark side. He became the most vicious pirate the seas had ever known.

HALF-BAKED AND TWICE-BAKED

CHAPTER SEVENTEEN

TWICE-BAKED'S STORY

For the next twelve years, BarbaRossa ruled the high seas. His reputation grew, and he became rich. His men were raiding towns and ships during the summer and resting in the bars of Zanzibar during the winter. He kept a distance from the crew while they were resting in Zanzibar. He didn't want to get involved with their ordinary affairs, and he spent most of his time with Abdi, whose political career had been ended by the rise of King Korsan.

One day, Half-Baked came to find him.

"Captain BarbaRossa, may I talk with you for a minute?"

"Go away, Half-Baked," said BarbaRossa, unwilling to hear yet another stupid idea. "I'm busy drinking with Abdi."

"But Captain, I recently met with somebody who had visited Gemlyk. You might be interested in talking to him."

"Who is this person?" barked BarbaRossa, suddenly interested.

"Well, Captain, it's my brother, Twice-Baked."

"What? All this time, you had a brother and you never mentioned him? He should have joined us on the *Falcon's Blood!*"

"I thought about inviting him to join our ship, he *is* a very strong man, but I decided not to bring him aboard."

"Why is that?" interrupted Abdi. "What was wrong with your brother?"

"I'm a little ashamed to admit it, but to tell you the truth, Twice-Baked isn't as smart as me, sir. He's about half as smart as me."

That made BarbaRossa laugh so hard, he started to cry. Abdi couldn't resist.

"If he's half as smart as Half-Baked, wouldn't he be called Quarter-Baked?"

"Well, Half-Baked, if he's half as smart as you, he'd be more than qualified to join the *Falcon's Blood,*" said BarbaRossa, wanting to relax his crew member. "Our ship isn't exactly full of sharp tools."

"What *is* your real name?" asked Abdi, and BarbaRossa ordered them another round of drinks. "Who gave you these nicknames?"

"They aren't nicknames, sir. Those are our real names!"

"What kind of parents would give such daring names to their kids?"

"Well, sir. Our father's name was Ian."

"Okay, that's a normal name."

"But nobody called him Ian! He was called Well-Done."

"Why was he called Well-Done?"

"He made the best barbecue in town! The whole neighborhood lined up at his parties every weekend. He became so good at smoking beef, they started to call him Well-Done. Nobody even knew his real name.

"Twice-Baked is my twin. My mom told me that I didn't stay in her tummy long enough. I came to this world too early. I was kind of half-baked, so that's what they named me. Twice-Baked, on the other hand, stayed in my mom's tummy for about twelve months. They had to force him out of there!

"Since I turned out to be a very smart kid with a cool name, my parents wanted my brother to be four times as successful as me. So, they named him Twice-Baked."

"But how come Twice-Baked isn't as smart as you?" Abdi asked.

"I don't know, sir. You'd expect him to be smarter, but he didn't turn out that way. But my parents didn't stop there. I have another younger brother."

"Is he here as well?"

"No. My youngest brother, Rui, turned out to be really stupid. He would never qualify as a pirate, so he went to a school. I think he graduated and became a guru, whatever that means. That was dumb. Look at me; I'm really thriving. I'm making tons of money, traveling all over the world, and partying with cool guys like you."

"Everything makes sense now," laughed Abdi. "And what kind of cookie is your mom?"

"She's not a cookie, sir. Her name is Cherie. We call her Cherry-on-Top."

"You got yourself a hell of a family, Half-Baked," said BarbaRossa, but he didn't choose to mention that he knew Rui, or that he had firsthand knowledge of his education. "Why don't you call Twice-Baked here? Let's hear what he knows about my old town."

Half-Baked called for his brother, who came over and sat with the pirates.

"I heard that you may have some news for me," said BarbaRossa. "Tell me what you know."

"Of course, Captain. I'm not sure whether I have good news or bad news, so please don't punish me, okay? After your raid, there weren't many people left in your village, but I did meet a Jynx woman named Yan Lu. She claimed that you stole her babies, and that the entire village hated you even before you raided them. They kicked your wife out of the village. I hope I'm not giving you bad news, Captain."

"No, Twice-Baked. I already knew this."

"Oh, then I can relax a little," Twice-Baked said. "Yan Lu wasn't a happy woman. She talked a lot about how unfair it was that your wife and your son are still enjoying their lives in the Altay Mountains, while she has been separated from her children."

BarbaRossa froze, then he drained his drink and grabbed Twice-Baked by the throat.

"Are you telling me my wife and son are alive?"

"Yes, Captain. Why are you choking me? I thought *this* would be the good news!"

BarbaRossa couldn't believe it. He jumped on the table.

"My love is alive! My son is alive! Set course for the Altay Mountains right away!"

Abdi had a different idea.

"The Altay mountains are in Jynx country. You can't climb those mountains with your wooden leg. You aren't young anymore, and you don't even know if these rumors are true. I think we should send a small expedition team first."

"What do you have in mind, Abdi?"

"I suggest we send a strong Jynx who can easily navigate the Altay Mountains. Zamora would fit the bill."

"Abdi, you are a wise man, but I am not sure about trusting Zamora."

"Offer to give him the *Falcon's Blood* if he brings back Benice and your son. He will be happy to check every hidden cove of the Altay Mountains in return for the promise of the ship."

"Okay. Bring Zamora here."

Abdi found Zamora relaxing in a bar next door.

"It looks like you are bored from inaction in this town. I have an interesting job for you."

"Go away, Abdi. I am doing fine here."

"You are going to like this. BarbaRossa just heard a rumor that his wife and son are alive and living in the Altay Mountains. BarbaRossa wants you to find her."

"Are you kidding me? I wouldn't lift a finger for that man."

"What if I tell you that if you play your cards right, you will have a chance to get rid of BarbaRossa and get the *Falcon's Blood* back?"

Zamora tilted towards Abdi. "Carry on. It sounds like you also want something for yourself from this mission."

"Yes. I want you to come back empty handed, if she is alive."

"You want Benice to disappear?"

"You *are* quick."

"I thought you were BarbaRossa's best friend."

"Perhaps once, but no more."

"What has changed?" Zamora asked suspiciously.

Abdi wondered whether to tell the pirate brute the whole story.

"You've lived in his shadow for a long time, now," he said eventually. "Do you think it's any easier for me? We both began with nothing and built a life of success and power. But that doesn't mean I want to answer to a half-man for the rest of my life."

"This, I understand," growled Zamora. Now that he trusted Abdi, the prospect of taking revenge on BarbaRossa intrigued him. "This sounds like my kind of mission. I will be happy to go to the Altay Mountains and come back empty handed."

They found BarbaRossa already celebrating with the rest of the crew.

"I am going to put an end to his happiness," Zamora whispered.

"Hey, BarbaRossa. Zamora accepts the challenge!" Abdi declared. "He will bring Benice and your son back."

Everybody in the bar cheered. They all thought the feud between BarbaRossa and Zamora was coming to an end.

Little Fan Fan stopped his dance.

"I want to go with Zamora," cried Little Fan Fan. "I have always wanted to see Jynx country."

"Sure. Zamora, take Little Fan Fan and Giant Yang Yang with you. They've been eager to visit the outside world."

Zamora looked towards Abdi and made a decapitation gesture, asking permission to kill the twins as well, but Abdi shook his head.

"Well, my life is not getting any easier," Zamora whispered, then he turned towards the twins. "Get ready to leave tomorrow morning. This is going to be a long journey, and there'll be no bickering while you're with me."

ALTAY MOUNTAINS

CHAPTER EIGHTEEN

VISITORS FOR MRS. BENICE

Zamora was happy to make a trip to his homeland. He followed BarbaRossa's instructions, taking Little Fan Fan and Giant Yang Yang with him into the mountains of Altay. The going was tough but, in the end, they found our home in the mountains and knocked on our door in disguise.

"Hello, ma'am," Zamora said. "I'm traveling with my two little boys. I decided to cut through the mountains, but I'm beginning to regret my decision. We're growing tired, and I don't know where we can safely rest. Could we stay at your house? Unfortunately, we don't have any money, but I'm strong. My boys could play with your son, and I could do some work around the house for you."

My mom was hesitant at first, so she quizzed him.

"Which two boys? I only see one boy, and he doesn't look like you."

Zamora was upset to discover that Giant Yang Yang was missing.

"No, they don't look like me. I adopted them when they were really young." He turned his attention to Little Fan Fan. "Where's your brother? What a naughty boy, he always disappears at the wrong time!"

Looking around, they saw Giant Yang Yang in the distance, standing behind a bush. Little Fan Fan yelled at him to join them, and Giant Yang Yang emerged from behind the bush. He pulled his zipper up, smiled with satisfaction, and walked toward them.

"What were you doing there, behind the bush?" asked my mom.

"He was *jungle juicing*," giggled Little Fan Fan, who knew exactly what was going on. Giant Yang Yang was still smiling.

"I'm sorry, ma'am. I was trying to help the environment." He tried to look as cute as possible. "Watering the bushes. You know, emergency."

"Wipe that smirk from your face," said my mom, not wanting to hear any more details. "Just get inside, and wash your hands." She allowed them into our house.

She was a cautious woman, but she had good reason to let them in. Her journey into the mountains had been treacherous but, climbing as high as she dared, she had been stunned to find a small cottage. An old man lived inside – he had been a lumberjack, once, but now he was old and struggled to care for himself. He only lived a few months more, but my mom cared for him, and he left her the cottage, as well as lots of advice about surviving in the mountains. She always said we were alive thanks to his kindness, and that it was our job to pass it on. Besides, there was a lot of work a strong man could do for us.

I quickly befriended Little Fan Fan and Giant Yang Yang.

The next day, we were relaxing at the barn, and Little Fan Fan asked, "Where's your father? We haven't seen him around."

"It's a long story, guys. I never met my father. He left home before I was born! He went to find medicine for my mom and never came back."

"Orion, you're still luckier than we are," said Giant Yang Yang. "We never met our father *or* our mother. We were brought to a ship when we were babies."

"I thought Zamora was your father."

"No, he's not. We think he may be the reason we were separated from our parents! All we really know is that he brought us to the ship."

"If you never met your parents, how do you know all this?"

"There was an older kid named Guru on our ship. He's very close to our captain, BarbaRossa. He got the information from him."

"Wait a minute," I interrupted. "Your captain's name is

BarbaRossa? Is he an Orhun with one eye, one hand, and one leg?"

"Yes," replied Little Fan Fan.

"I can't believe this," I said, my eyes sparkling. That was a monumental moment in my life. I never knew my father was alive up to that point. "I am certain that your captain is my father. Oh! I'll go to Zamora right away and demand he take me to my father."

"You need to be very cautious, Orion." Giant Yang Yang tried to calm me down. "I'm afraid we didn't tell you the whole truth."

"What are you hiding from me?" I asked.

"We aren't just regular travelers crossing the mountains. We're pirates. Zamora is pretending to be a decent person, but he is the most vicious of our pirate crew."

After the twins told me everything they knew about BarbaRossa, I assessed the situation.

"I understand that Zamora isn't a good guy, but in order to find my father, I have no choice but to confront him. We don't even know why Zamora came here. He might just disappear as quickly as he arrived. I can't let this opportunity pass me by."

I looked out the window. Zamora was chopping wood without his shirt, and I saw the letter "B" on his back. We went outside and started to probe him.

"That's a cool tattoo you've got on your back, Mr. Zamora. How did you get it? What does the letter 'B' stand for?" I asked.

Zamora didn't answer.

"He got it from BarbaRossa," said Little Fan Fan, and Zamora immediately realized there was something going on.

"That's interesting… my father's name was also BarbaRossa! Does the man that gave you the tattoo have one eye, one hand, and one leg, Mr. Zamora?"

"Yes!" cried Little Fan Fan, continuing to reveal more information for Zamora. "What a coincidence; our BarbaRossa only has one eye, one hand, and one leg."

Zamora froze. His secret was out! He pulled out his knife and took me, Little Fan Fan, and Giant Yang Yang to the barn.

"Now, you listen to me, little boy. It's true that your father gave me the tattoo. Now, I'm going to give one to you."

"Do it, I dare you! My father will make you pay for it," I replied. "Where is he? I want to see him!"

"You will never see him, little boy. He sent me to bring you and your mom to him, but he made a mistake," growled Zamora.

Little Fan Fan couldn't stand Zamora's cruelty, but he spoke beyond his years.

"Stop it, Zamora! You're not going to kill Orion. If you kill him, I'll tell BarbaRossa. He won't like that you killed his son."

Zamora tried to think of a solution. I'm sure he thought about killing all of us, but it would have been too suspicious to return to the *Falcon's Blood* alone, even if he could make it back down the mountain without help.

"Okay, I won't kill this boy and his mother. But, in return, you're not going to tell BarbaRossa that we found them."

"Give the pirate oath right now," said Little Fan Fan.

"Okay," said Zamora, weighing up his options. "I give you my oath! I'm not going to kill anybody. But, in return, you'll swear the pirate oath to *me* that you won't tell BarbaRossa what we found."

Reluctantly, they swore the oath, and Zamora grinned.

"Pack up everything, right now! We're leaving."

Zamora pushed the children aside and stormed into the living room, where he grabbed one of my old pictures. He told my mom that they had an emergency and had to leave immediately.

Little Fan Fan and Giant Yang Yang felt guilty about the deal they'd made with Zamora, but it was the best they could do to save everybody's life. I realized that the time had come to say goodbye to my friends and rushed to my room to get gifts for the twins.

"Take my parrot with you! Her name is Beacon. When the time is right for me to meet with my father, strap a message to Beacon's leg. She's a very smart parrot, and she'll be able to find me no matter where you release her. Beacon will bring your message to me."

Thinking about my mum's philosophy, I also gave them a tiny

bottle the old lumberjack had left behind. Giant Yang Yang opened the gift and saw that it was a little bottle of Culligan's Mustache Juice.

"Apply this above your lip, every day," I said. "It's guaranteed to give you a mustache, regardless of how old you are."

Little Fan Fan and Giant Yang Yang promised me that they would help me find my dad. In return, I promised the twins I'd help find their parents. After we exchanged gifts, they departed, and my mom never understood why they had really visited or why they were leaving the house.

ORION AND BEACON

CHAPTER NINETEEN

MEETING
AT GEMLYK

I didn't hear from the twins for several years. I thought they had forgotten about me, and I stayed at home to help my mother. Though she had surprised even herself by living for so many years, she was getting sicker every day; she needed that Zanzibar Elixir more than ever. The pristine mountain air had kept her alive for longer than anyone could have hoped, but she was now close to death.

I was hopeless. I wanted to search for my father, but there was no way I could leave my mom. One day, I was chopping wood in the forest when a bird flew over my head and landed on the branches above.

"Attention!" it said. "I have a message to Orion from Little Fan Fan and Giant Yang Yang. Attention! I have a message to Orion from Little Fan Fan and Giant Yang Yang."

Beacon flew around me once and then landed in my hands. I gently grabbed Beacon's leg and removed a message. Indeed, it was a letter from the twins.

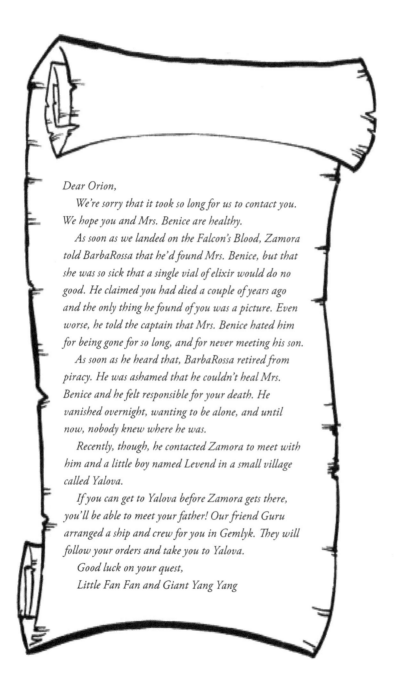

Dear Orion,

   We're sorry that it took so long for us to contact you. We hope you and Mrs. Benice are healthy.

   As soon as we landed on the Falcon's Blood, Zamora told BarbaRossa that he'd found Mrs. Benice, but that she was so sick that a single vial of elixir would do no good. He claimed you had died a couple of years ago and the only thing he found of you was a picture. Even worse, he told the captain that Mrs. Benice hated him for being gone for so long, and for never meeting his son.

   As soon as he heard that, BarbaRossa retired from piracy. He was ashamed that he couldn't heal Mrs. Benice and he felt responsible for your death. He vanished overnight, wanting to be alone, and until now, nobody knew where he was.

   Recently, though, he contacted Zamora to meet with him and a little boy named Levend in a small village called Yalova.

   If you can get to Yalova before Zamora gets there, you'll be able to meet your father! Our friend Guru arranged a ship and crew for you in Gemlyk. They will follow your orders and take you to Yalova.

   Good luck on your quest,
   Little Fan Fan and Giant Yang Yang

I finally had my chance! My friendship with Little Fan Fan and Giant Yang Yang had paid off. I asked permission from my mom to leave home, though I didn't tell her that my dad was alive. I didn't want to bother her until I actually found my dad, especially since I didn't know if I'd be able to bring him home safely. My mom didn't ask a single question; she could see the spark in my eyes, and she knew this quest was my destiny, so she gave me permission with one condition.

"No matter what you do out there, I want you to come back. Okay? I don't want to look at the stars by myself every night."

I came down from the mountains of Altay and made it back to Gemlyk. The whole town was abandoned, except for an old Jynx couple who sat gazing hopelessly out to sea. I heard them talking about their twin boys and was amazed to hear them use the names Fan Fan and Yang Yang.

"I am Orion," I said to them. "May I ask your names?"

"I am Yan Lu," said the woman. "This is my husband, Hao Wu."

"Mrs. Lu and Mr. Wu, do you see that ship over there?"

"Yes. That looks like a pirate ship, to me," said Mr. Wu.

"It is indeed a pirate ship. We have to get on that ship quickly. I don't have much time to explain, but I want you to trust me."

"What are you talking about, young boy?" asked Mr. Wu.

"I think I know where your children are," I said, knowing that I was gambling with this old couple's lives. "I can help you find them."

As soon as she heard the news, Mrs. Lu fainted, while Mr. Wu jumped up from his seat and grabbed me in a headlock! I couldn't breathe and started turning purple.

"Don't mess with parents with broken hearts! How dare you jump in front of my wife and tell her something like this?

"你疯了吗？怎么能对我太太这样唐突、随意信口雌黄，让她再次心碎!"

"Now, I'm going to release my grip a tiny bit so you can talk. Tell me everything you know. If you don't convince me you're telling the truth, you're a dead boy."

"I can't prove that I met your children," I said, coughing, "but I met twin Jynx boys who were stolen by pirates and go by Giant Yang Yang and Little Fan Fan. This can't be a coincidence! You have to trust me. Don't let Mrs. Lu wake up to a missed chance. I can take you to your children; they're my friends. What do you have to lose?"

"Yes, you're right," said Mr. Wu, relaxing his grip. "We've been waiting here all these years, but nothing has ever happened."

"Thank you, Mr. Wu. I hope this will work – for your and your children's sake."

Mr. Wu and Mrs. Lu boarded my ship, and we sailed here. We hoped to find Levend and BarbaRossa in Yalova, before they left to meet Zamora. Of course, I still needed to explain who BarbaRossa was, which would certainly get me killed by Mr. Wu.

AYSHIN, ZHU ZHU, AND ZHEN ZHEN RECOVERING ZANZIBAR TREASURE

CHAPTER TWENTY

RESCUE MISSION

'd told Ayshin and Auntie Aysun everything I knew about BarbaRossa, and now I had to find out why BarbaRossa had taken Levend to the *Falcon's Blood*.

"Ayshin, listen to me carefully now," I said. "I was disappointed that I couldn't find my dad or Levend in Yalova, but I found you. I told you my entire story, and I hope I've earned your trust. If you help me find my father, and help my dear friends Little Fan Fan and Giant Yang Yang join their parents, I will help you find Levend. Tell me what's going on, so we can find your brother."

I knew Ayshin held the key to the mystery. Ayshin knew Auntie Aysun wouldn't be happy, and might even blame her for Levend's kidnapping, but she had no choice but to trust me. Ayshin looked at Auntie Aysun, and without asking for her permission, she began talking.

"You're right, Orion. Your father lived in this town for the last three, maybe four, years. We always suspected him of being a pirate; he didn't talk to anybody, he was quiet, but he was a very good fisherman. For some reason, he liked Levend. They went fishing together, occasionally."

"How long ago did Levend and my dad meet?"

"I think about two years, but they only started fishing recently."

"Think about it, Ayshin. What changed after two years? Why would my dad suddenly decide to contact Zamora? There must be something."

Of course, Ayshin knew exactly what it was. She looked at Auntie Aysun.

"It was his seabubble," she said.

"Seabubble?" I asked. "What's a seabubble?"

"That was the secret that triggered your dad contacting Zamora."

"What can this seabubble do?" I asked, and Auntie Aysun nodded in agreement.

Ayshin confessed, telling us exactly how the seabubble worked. Auntie Aysun was upset that the kids had kept it a secret, but I was already putting all the clues together.

"Of course!" I shouted. "BarbaRossa must be trying to recover the lost Zanzibar Elixir. They'll be heading to the shipwreck site! Quickly, when did Levend disappear?"

"Just yesterday."

"My ship is much faster than Zamora's! Now, listen, I have a plan. But Ayshin, please, please, please tell me you have an extra seabubble."

Ayshin clenched her teeth.

"Yes. We do," she confessed hesitantly. "In fact, we have three of them."

"Bring them to me."

"Of course. But... there's a problem."

"What's that?"

"The seabubbles were custom-made. They can only fit me, Zhu Zhu, and Zhen Zhen."

"Then you're coming with me as well!"

"Hmm, I don't think so," corrected Auntie Aysun.

"With the permission of your aunt, of course," I added.

"I already lost Levend to the pirates," said Auntie Aysun. "I'm not prepared to lose Ayshin as well." I froze; there was nothing I could say, but Auntie Aysun wasn't finished. "Of course, that means I have to come with you."

"We're coming to rescue Levend as well," said Zhu Zhu. "We want to help Ayshin!"

"I'll prepare you the ladies' quarters of the ship," I said. "I hope that I've earned your trust. I am a good man, I swear. I *will* help you save Levend, but you must trust my plans. I know how to get to the shipwreck site. It's close to Zanzibar, and my ship is fast. We can arrive much earlier than Zamora's ship if we leave right now. So, chop chop, let's go!"

Indeed, we arrived at the shipwreck long before the *Falcon's Blood*. I dropped anchor and started to give instructions to Ayshin, Zhu Zhu, and Zhen Zhen.

"Girls, this is the most dangerous task you've ever had. There are sharks and lobster-popsters in the Zanzibar waters; it's not like swimming in the calm waters of Yalova. You need to finish the task as soon as possible, before they awake and attack you. There are a bunch of chests with letters on them in the shipwreck. The elixirs are in the chests with gold letters. Do not waste time with the other chests. Do you understand me?"

I wasn't comfortable sending the girls to the shipwreck, but this mission wasn't just about my father or mother anymore. We had to recover and trade the treasure with Zamora to save Levend.

Ayshin, Zhu Zhu, and Zhen Zhen didn't hesitate. They put their seabubbles on and dove to the seabed. There, they found the shipwreck, and we brought up the treasure chests with gold letters. One by one, they emptied the treasure chests, but they couldn't find the elixir. I was disappointed but still determined.

"Girls, go back in the water and collect the remaining treasure chests. Maybe Little Fan Fan and Giant Yang Yang gave me the wrong information about the letters on the chests."

Just before the girls could begin their second diving campaign, the crew on the mast yelled, "Alarm, alarm, alarm! There's a pirate ship on the horizon!"

"Lock these six treasure chests and return them to the water," I ordered.

"Why would we do that?" Zhen Zhen asked.

"We *want* Zamora to find the chests. Otherwise, he has no reason to keep my dad and Levend around."

"Pack up and run away," I shouted. "We can't face Zamora's men."

I moved my ship to a safe distance from the *Falcon's Blood* and watched their approach. I saw that they were pulling the treasure chests out of the water. They would be in for a surprise when they discovered the chests had been emptied! It was a long time before I realized the *Falcon's Blood* was standing still. Nobody was steering it; something was wrong with the ship.

In the meantime, Ayshin, Zhu Zhu, Zhen Zhen, Auntie Aysun, and the twins' parents were waiting anxiously.

"It's time," I ordered. "It's time to go to the *Falcon's Blood*. If our loved ones are alive, now is the time to save them."

As we got closer to the *Falcon's Blood*, we saw the carnage. The deck was littered with dead pirates, and Ayshin started to cry. While my crew tied the ships together and built a gangway, I found a rope and swung across to the *Falcon's Blood*. That's where I met Mr. Levend for the first time.

"So, all of your friends got together on the *Falcon's Blood*!" cries one of the Yalova kids. "That's amazing. What happened to Mr. Ben?"

"I think it's better for Mr. Levend to tell you what happened on the *Falcon's Blood.*"

"Mr. Levend, please tell us what happened to Mr. Ben. Did he survive? You told us he was going to give you a treasure. Did you get the treasure?"

"Thank you, Mr. Orion," I say, taking his place in front of the crowd. "I will be happy to tell you everything, kids."

ORION MEETS BARBAROSSA

CHAPTER TWENTY-ONE

BARBAROSSA'S SECRET

was still none the wiser as to why Orion had boarded the *Falcon's Blood* and seemed to know everyone aboard. Raising the binoculars to look at his ship, I saw an old couple. The woman seemed happy, though she wasn't quite celebrating yet, while her husband was crying!

Who are these people yelling from the other ship? How do they know my name? I asked myself. I moved my gaze a little, and I couldn't believe what I was seeing. It was Auntie Aysun, Ayshin, and her best friends Zhu Zhu and Zhen Zhen!

"Hoppalaa! How did *you* get here?" I cried out in disbelief.

Ayshin found a rope and swung across to the *Falcon's Blood*. I caught her in the air and, before I knew it, I was hugging my sister. Once she knew I was okay, she broke away from me and ran to Orion.

"How's your dad?"

"He's not doing well, Ayshin. He sustained heavy injuries."

"Did you talk to him?"

"No. He couldn't open his eyes."

"Wait a minute," I said. "You're BarbaRossa's son? I can't believe it! He thought you were dead!"

"I know. Zamora lied," Orion agreed. Overwhelmed by the time lost with his father, he began to sob.

"I know it may not be much consolation," I said, "but I did spend some good times with him. He loved me… like a son. He told me that I looked like you."

Little Fan Fan and Giant Yang Yang were watching the elderly Jynx couple swing across from their ship. The four of them stood facing each other, and there was a brief moment of silence. The kids didn't need any explanation; with one look at their parents, they knew who they were meeting. Little Fan Fan and Giant Yang Yang hugged their mom. It was an embrace they'd been waiting fourteen years to have. Their father wrapped his arms around them; the Wu family was joined together at last.

All eight kids gathered around BarbaRossa, with me and Orion kneeling down on either side of him. He recognized me, reaching out to grasp my hand. Guru approached from behind, grabbing under BarbaRossa's arms and lifting him up. Little Fan Fan and Giant Yang Yang stood next to me, their parents' hands on their shoulders, and the girls stood in front of BarbaRossa, protecting him from the sun.

"BarbaRossa," I said softly, "you have a visitor. The boy holding your other hand is your son, Orion."

"My love, you are alive," he said. "No words can describe how much I missed you. I thought I'd never hold your hand. How is your mother? How is my Benice?"

"She's not well, Dad. She survived, but she's been sick since you left."

"Kids, I'm glad to hold both of your hands at the same time. I want to see my love Benice more than anything, right now, but I may not have much time left. I never knew whether I was blessed or cursed with love and friendship. I found true love but couldn't protect it, I had a best friend but he betrayed me. I was too quick to fall to the dark side. I don't want you to ever lose your faith in love and friendship.

"I will give each of you a treasure; the most important thing you will ever have in your entire lives."

Orion and I looked at each other. The treasure chests were empty. He couldn't make either one of us any richer. What else could he give us?

"Orion," he continued, "I will start with you. Go to the treasure chest marked with the letter 'C'. Close the chest lid and push on the letter 'C' while opening the chest. A hidden compartment should pop out from the side of the chest, and inside that is a small key."

Orion did exactly as he was told. *No wonder I couldn't find the key when I recovered the chests the first time,* he thought. Then, he shouted to his dad.

"Dad, I found the key. What do you want me to do next?"

"Close each and every one of the chests," said BarbaRossa, and Orion did as he was asked. "Now, open the chests with the new key."

Orion closed the lids and unlocked the chests. Instead of the main lid, a secret compartment opened from the bottom.

"Now, collect everything inside those hidden compartments."

Each of the hidden compartments contained a vial in which a blue, glue-like substance sloshed around. Orion collected the elixirs from all six chests.

"Orion, that liquid is the Zanzibar Elixir. Your mom needs that elixir to get better. I collected the nectar years ago, but unfortunately I couldn't take it to your mom. You can."

"You're right, Father. Healing Mom is the best treasure I will ever get in my life. I will take this medicine to her. I will tell her that you always loved her."

BarbaRossa tried to turn his face toward Guru, but he was too weak.

"Rui, come to the front. Let me see your face. You're a smart kid. Your apprenticeship aboard the *Falcon's Blood* is now complete. Here, you have seen the dark side of humanity, and you have developed a strong character. My gift to you was to teach you the workings of the dark side. Now, the time has come for you to conquer the rest of the world."

"But—" began Guru, but BarbaRossa shook his head.

"In a moment," he said, "I'll be true to my word, trust me. But Levend, it's your turn now. Come here. Who are those little girls over there?"

"That's my sister, Ayshin, and her best friends Zhu Zhu and Zhen Zhen."

"Ayshin, Zhu Zhu, Zhen Zhen, Little Fan Fan, Giant Yang Yang, all of you kids, come close to me. I'm glad to see all of you together, holding hands. It looks like you're good friends."

Little Fan Fan told me later that, in that moment, he was remembering my words.

You can't ask for true friendship, because it's not something any-one can just give. It grows over time. You share experiences, you play together, you help each other through the hard times. Then, one day, you're looking back on those memories and you realize you have it and that you wouldn't trade it for anything.

BarbaRossa's gentle voice interrupted Little Fan Fan's daydream.

"Now, Ayshin, go to the treasure chests and stand between the chests with letters 'E' and 'N'."

I was surprised. He still wanted to give us something from these chests, even though there was nothing left. No money, no gold, no silver, not even precious elixir. What else could he give us?

Ayshin went to the treasure chests, which were neatly arranged to spell "BENICE."

"You spelled your wife's name with the treasure chests. I know you loved her very much," Ayshin said.

"Now," said BarbaRossa, gesturing to Ayshin, "sit between the two chests and push them apart."

"Why?" Ayshin asked.

"I don't have much time, Ayshin. Please do it exactly as I told you. I'm going to give you the secret to a happy life."

Ayshin sat between the two chests, putting her back against "E" and pushing "N" away with her legs. The chests moved apart, but nothing else seemed to happen. BarbaRossa waved us all closer.

"Thank you, Ayshin. You can come back here now. Unfortunately, I can't give you any more money, but I can give you the biggest treasure of your life. I want you all to grow old and happy."

What did he mean? What was the treasure he was giving us? All of the treasure chests were empty. I turned around and looked at the chests. Now the chests with the letters "E" and "N" were pushed apart, the six chests spelled out two words.

BE   NICE

I was shocked. The secret message of life he was giving us was "Be nice."

I looked at my friends. They were all in tears. All eight kids held hands. Only a few lucky people in the whole world have true friendship, and we knew we were among them.

AYSHIN'S SPECIAL DAY AT THE ISKELE

EPILOGUE

As I finish explaining how BarbaRossa gave us our treasure, the Yalova kids are holding hands and silently crying about their beloved Mr. Ben.

"Kids, you won't see Mr. Ben tomorrow, but it shouldn't be very hard for you to imagine that his spirit will be there with us. I want you to understand that while I, Orion, and all our friends at the party belong to his legacy, so do all the kids of Yalova."

The kids thank us for sharing Mr. Ben's story, and Cem comes forward.

"Mr. Levend, I have a request. Remember I told you that you can take *Eyass* if you want? I changed my mind. I would like to keep *Eyass* exactly where it is. I think it would be more fitting for Yalova's kids to take care of *Eyass* and pass Mr. Ben's message on from one generation to the next."

"You are wise beyond your age," I reply. "I'd be happy to leave

Eyass in your care. Now, don't forget the party tomorrow. All Yalova's kids are invited, okay?"

The kids disperse, and Orion and I walk down the beach.

"It's a sweet story," he says, "but do you think they'd feel the same way about it if they knew what happened afterward?"

"They should," I reply. "There's no greater story than the friendships we make in life."

"If only all our friends would be here, tomorrow."

"It's a big day," I agree, "but it's not the end of our lives or our friendships. Maybe we'll all be together again, eventually."

"Really?" Orion asks, surprised. "You could forgive and forget, just like that?"

"Yes, I could. I'd forgive without any hesitation. BarbaRossa never came back to apologize to Mrs. Benice, and he deprived her of seeing him again. She'd have rather died young in his arms than grow old alone. I loved BarbaRossa, but I don't want to follow his path, and that's not what he wanted for any of us, either."

"Well, maybe we will all be together tomorrow," says Orion. "Maybe we'll see a speck on the horizon, at least, if pride doesn't get in the way."

"Is being proud more important than your friends?"

"To some," Orion says. "We all saw my father's message, that day, but perhaps it wasn't enough for some of us. Or maybe you're right; perhaps it will be, in time."

We look out to sea for a minute, sharing our silent bond as the sons of BarbaRossa.

"I should get some rest," Orion says. "I don't want to be tired for your sister's big day."

"I suppose not," I sigh, my medals heavy on my chest. "Not after everything we've been through so that it could happen."

"A story for another day," says Orion, "and another group of rascally children. I'll see you tomorrow, my friend."

He leaves me standing at the iskele, back where it all started. Tomorrow, all eyes will be on Ayshin. The iskele will be full, the people cheering when she appears. She'll be accompanied by the most important women in our life: Mrs. Benice on her right and Auntie Aysun on her left. Both will be beaming, proud that such a day has come. Her friends, Zhu Zhu and Zhen Zhen, will walk behind her.

I stare at the horizon, searching for the black speck that Orion described. A ship, far distant, that might come closer and closer, bringing us all back together.

"Be brave, and thoughtful, and sly, and courageous, and cunning, and forthright," I say to the imagined vessel. "But for his sake, above all of that, be nice."

I wait for a while, but I don't see anything. Not yet, anyway. Eventually, I grow tired, and I make my way to bed, looking forward to a wonderful day spent with my friends and family.

CPSIA information can be obtained
at www.ICGtesting.com
Printed in the USA
LVHW071809110319
610164LV00031B/339/P